Pop Fiction:
Stories Inspired By Songs

Various Artists

Published in 2010 by YouWriteOn Publishing

Copyright © Individual copyright belongs to each of the writers included in this collection for their own individual stories, 2010

First Edition

The authors assert their moral rights under the Copyright, Designs and Patents Act, 1988, to be identified as the authors of this work.

All Rights reserved. No part of this publication may be reproduced, stored in a retrieval system, or transmitted, in any form or by any means, without the prior written consent of the publisher, nor be otherwise circulated in any form of binding or cover other that that in which it is published and without a similar condition being imposed on the subsequent purchaser.

British Library C.I.P.

A CIP catalogue record for this title is available from the British Library.

Acknowledgements

The authors of *Pop Fiction: Stories Inspired by Songs* would like to sing the praises of:

Ted Smith for his support

YouWriteOn.com, for making this collaboration possible – www.youwriteon.com

Stéphanie Thieullent @ NU Creative Ltd., for a perfect cover – www.thieuvite.com / www.nucreative.co.uk

Tom Rose, for swinging that typewriter with impeccable rhythm

Pennie Smith, for inspiring our front cover

And everyone involved in the songs featured in *Pop Fiction*, for – of course – the music.

Thank you.

Cover based on a photo of Paul Simonon, © Pennie Smith, used by kind permission.

Pop Fiction edited by Daniel Lewis, Lev Parikian and Tom Singleton.

Initial proceeds from *Pop Fiction* will be donated to Blue Lamp Foundation – www.bluelamp-foundation.org

Contents

Intro – Daniel Lewis……………………….……………9

The Symbiosis Of Music And Literature – Marc Nash   15

Side One:

01. Cut And Run – Karen Snape-Williams………...……..21
Inspired by 'I Shot The Sheriff'
– Bob Marley & The Wailers

02. Watanabe's Honour – Tom Singleton……………….35
Inspired by '"Heroes"' – David Bowie

03. Disney's Dream Debased – Daniel Lewis.…………..53
Inspired by 'Disney's Dream Debased' – The Fall

04. Our Song – Marc Nash………………………………..69
Inspired by '"Heroes"' – David Bowie

05. Personal Study – Jacky Cowper……….……..……...83
Inspired by 'Tainted Love' – Soft Cell

06. The Other Side – Lee Williams……………..………93
Inspired by '"Heroes"' – David Bowie

07. A Life In The Day – Lev Parikian……………..……..105
Inspired by 'A Day In The Life' – The Beatles

08. The Taffeta Wall – Carole Pitt…………..…………..119
Inspired by '"Heroes"' – David Bowie

09. Where's Captain Kirk? – Aís…………...…………..137
Inspired by 'Where's Captain Kirk?' – Spizzenergi

Side Two:

01. Simon Sees – Jacky Cowper………..…………..…..151
Inspired by '"Heroes"' – David Bowie

02. Hotel C.N.S – Marc Nash……………………..………167
Inspired by 'IY' – 23 Skidoo

03. The Canadian – Karen Snape-Williams…..……….185
Inspired by '"Heroes"' – David Bowie

04. Diamonds And Rust – Carole Pitt…..…….………..207
Inspired by 'Diamonds And Rust' – Joan Baez

05. The Only Conclusion – Daniel Lewis……………..…..225
Inspired by '"Heroes"' – David Bowie

06. Interception – Tom Singleton……………………….239
Inspired by '(White Man) In Hammersmith Palais' – The Clash

07. Heroes For A Day – Aís……………..…………….255
Inspired by '"Heroes"' – David Bowie

08. Let's Get Physical! – Lee Williams…..……………..285
Inspired by 'Physical' – Olivia Newton-John

09. Heroes – Lev Parikian……………...……….………..291
Inspired by '"Heroes"' – David Bowie

Intro

Daniel Lewis

Just as a perfectly-formed sentence sends shivers down the spine, so a certain song swells the heart as it reminds you of everything you failed to do when you were nineteen. And just as an intriguing plot draws you into a world you never thought you'd love, so that difficult third album reveals itself to be multilayered and magnificent on its sixth listen.

I call myself a writer, and yet I'm defined by noise; my life is one long *Original Soundtrack*: a compilation burnt with only me in mind. Literature and music are equally essential to me, and when they swirl together and impact on each other…I believe the results can be exhilarating.

Which is why I – music obsessive, literature lover – scissor-jumped at the opportunity to be involved with the compilation you now hold in your hands.

Pop Fiction: Stories Inspired by Songs owes its existence to three S's: Singleton, Smith and Strummer. In October 2009, Tom Singleton posted 'Interception' on the Arts Council-funded site, YouWriteOn.com, managed by the tireless Ted Smith. The tale was influenced by The

Clash's superlative '(White Man) In Hammersmith Palais' – or, to be pedantic, Joe Strummer's lyrics. Tom then mentioned his story on YouWriteOn.com's message board, and asked if other authors active on the site would be interested in writing stories inspired by songs, with a view to self-publishing the results in a collection.

Nine writers committed, and we agreed the format early on: to each contribute two stories; one based on a song of our choice, and one influenced by a specific song, to be collectively agreed. Our readers would not only enjoy tales tied to a range of artists, drawing on punk, rock, pop, reggae and country, but also experience nine interpretations of a single tune, which we all determined should be David Bowie's '"Heroes"'.

YouWriteOn.com played a major part in making this project a reality. The site has, since its inception in 2006, provided a free online platform for aspiring authors to upload their writing, reach an audience and – most importantly – hone their talents, via constructive feedback from fellow writers' reviews. It offered a forum for us to discover each others' writing and, via its message board, Tom's inspired idea. In addition, YouWriteOn.com also provided a painless route to self-publishing, without which *Pop Fiction* would probably still be an idea as opposed to a fully-realised collection of killer tunes. As a result, the nine of us have embraced the D.I.Y. aesthetic – like our punk precursors – and pushed *Pop Fiction* into existence.

Aside from YouWriteOn.com, I'd also like to thank Pennie Smith for granting permission to adapt her photograph of Paul Simonon for *Pop Fiction*. A great book deserves a great cover and, for us *Pop Fiction*ers, it made sense that a set of stories inspired by songs should salute an album on its sleeve. Pennie's original photo – framed within Ray Lowry's day-glo Elvis-style lettering for The Clash's seminal *London Calling* – isn't an album cover; it's rock 'n' roll. An iconic moment of creation and destruction, captured forever.

We're as proud of our cover version as the stories themselves, so I'd like to thank the gifted Stéphanie Thieullent for creating such an effective homage.

*

Reading these stories, it's intriguing to observe how different authors have responded to *Pop Fiction*'s premise. Some have taken the literal approach, let their chosen songs seep into the stories themselves. Others have used titles or particular lyrics as their springboard. And a few haven't referenced their source material at all; the essence of their song is powerful enough to inspire another world. Three-minute marvels re-imagined into three-thousand word contemporary classics.

As a result, *Pop Fiction* is the most eclectic mix

tape you'll ever receive, lovingly compiled. Here, you'll discover black comedy, psychological horror and skewed romance, as Spizzenergi, Soft Cell and 23 Skidoo (hopefully) seduce you in the background.

But rather than focus on interpretations of different songs, it's worthwhile comparing the stories inspired by our collective choice, '"Heroes"'. In its most literal reading, Bowie's tale is one of triumph over adversity, of hope, celebration and resilience. It's a classic love song, full of worship and dedication. And, yet, '"Heroes"' cuts deeper. Bowie's lyrics allude to time running out. As the passion in his voice grows, so does his sense of desperation. Mix such a powerful performance with that other-worldly, reverb-drenched tune, and you've got a song to stir the hardest heart. Personally, I'd argue that if '"Heroes"' doesn't touch your heart, it's no longer beating…but that's my biased opinion. And surely that's the point: these songs, and their interpretations, are all individual. Are Bowie's '"Heroes"' free or doomed? Will their love soar like the song's tune, or is this their last impassioned stand?

I'm not convinced it matters.

What's relevant about '"Heroes"' is that, here, the song inspires everything from light-hearted science fiction to elegiac ghost story. What makes a hero is, like so much, subjective.

At the same time, themes unite us as writers: four versions deal with war, whilst my story links thematically with Marc Nash and Lev Parikian's interpretations. And that's the power of a great song: it can inspire distinct voices and yet, somehow, compel us to write about the same subject. Even Bowie's iconic dolphins course their way through a few of these tales.

But, for all our attempts, can we actually do '"Heroes"', or any of these songs, justice? Can we really emulate the emotional power and excitement music inspires, using mere words?

I don't know. But we've tried.

And we'll try.

Because now, for your pleasure, it's time for us to take to the stage and perform.

So whack everything up to eleven, put on your best dancin' shoes, give *Pop Fiction* a spin…

…and let's rock.

The Symbiosis Of Music And Literature
Marc Nash

I never read books until I was fourteen years old. Typical boy, I was out in all weathers playing cricket or football instead. What tuned me into literature was a respected older cousin's suggestion to listen to The Cure's 'Killing An Arab' and then read Camus' *L'Étranger*, both of which I dutifully did. At the time I was on the look out for cool bands to drop in to conversations at school, but thanks to this one suggestion I had my appreciation opened up to a second vibrant art form.

Oh yeah, I not only read books now, I write 'em as well. And, as part of that, music is still key.

Literature is perhaps regarded as the highest, noblest art form for opening our minds towards contemplation of the world around us. And rock 'n' roll, bubble-gum three-minute-pop about puppy love and teenage crushes, is regarded in some quarters as the most disposable of art forms. Books occasionally percolate society's collective consciousness, for example the obscenity trials over *Lady Chatterley's Lover* or *Last Exit To Brooklyn*. Pop frequently outrages, from Elvis The Pelvis, through 'God Save The Queen' to Beastie Boys.

Yet, despite being from fairly opposite ends of art's 'brow' spectrum, the two are fundamentally intertwined and mutually inform one another.

Apart from the above example of The Cure, Gang of Four referenced Joseph Conrad's *Heart Of Darkness* with 'We Live As We Dream Alone' and Kafka's beetle from *Metamorphosis* in their song 'Anthrax'. Howard Devoto, singer in Magazine, referenced Raskolnikov and Dostoevsky's 'Underground Man' in 'Song From Under The Floorboards'. Just a few examples of artists honouring fellow artists who have gone before them. Inspired them. Given them words and ideas to stir their own creative pools...

Of course, it goes the other way too. Poets Linton Kwesi Johnson, Benjamin Zephaniah and John Cooper-Clarke have all performed live with backing bands. Gus Van Sant has set texts by William S. Burroughs to music, and Steve Fisk composed music for the late Steven Jesse Bernstein's poetry. Then there are the crossover artists: Patti Smith, Nick Cave and Henry Rollins to name but three with a foot firmly planted in both camps. Plus recently we have had short story anthologies inspired by the words of Mark E. Smith and the music of Sonic Youth.

So now nine new writers offer their contributions to the symbiosis; nine stories inspired by songs from different musical artists, plus nine stories arising from the same song: '"Heroes"' by David Bowie. Nine very different interpretations, no mere cover versions.

Side One:

Cut And Run

Karen Snape-Williams

Dear Lord,

I'm looking at the sky. A beautiful, blue Arizona sky. Not a cloud. Not a bird. Just blue. Couldn't be in no better place to appreciate the vista. What with lying here. In the dust and the dirt. In the middle of the street.

Last time we conversed, Lord, was the day we planted Pa. The day I sat in church puzzling as to why in hell everyone was sobbin', weepin' and bawlin'. Way I saw it, Pa was an evil son of a bitch. Thrashed me if I was good and beat me if I was bad. Didn't know if I was comin' or goin'.

"You done crashing around, Jeremiah? You woke me up, boy."

"Sorry, Pa."

"You fed those chickens?"

"Yes, sir."

"Milked the cow?"

"Yes, sir."

"Bacon smells good."

"Sure does, an' I got some oatmeal bubblin' on the stove. Made it just the way you like it, Pa."

"Oatmeal! I'm sick of darn oatmeal."

Wham!

With Ma dead some eight years and Pa now lying beside her, didn't take long for the bank to foreclose on the farm and for me to clear out. Been killin', stealin' and whorin' ever since.

Hitched a ride with a wagon train. Ten families. Hard-working folks from back east, rolling west and searching for a better life. Fine intentions but stupid.

Six days out, grumblin' about the dirt and the heat, they unhitched their wagons by a river and went bathing. Warned 'em about the flies and mosquitoes buzzing around their heads, but they didn't pay no heed. Didn't take long for disease to spread through the camp. Twenty miles out of Flagstaff they're sickin' up and hollerin' they want to stop. I told them nobody stops in Indian territory unless they're planning on dyin'.

Heard the whoopin' an hour later. High on the ridge above us, saw the line of Navajo warriors, two hundred or more, shrieking and yelling, waving their bows, tomahawks and rifles high in the air. Felt the sweat running down my spine. Felt my mouth go dry as a creek in high summer.

Man in charge ordered the wagons to form a circle as those Indians galloped down the ridge. War painted, feathered and furious, they were hell-bent on a massacre.

I got down low. Fired off a few shots with my rifle. With folks dropping all round me, I knew it was useless. Those Indians outnumbered us three to one.

There was a boy beside me. Big blue eyes. Fighting tears. Trying to be a man. Failing. In those few seconds, as women screamed and men died, I had to make a decision. The boy was twelve, maybe thirteen. Strong lookin'. Heavy. Knew he'd take some haulin' to his feet. It'd waste precious time and time was precious. Way I figured, we'd both die.

I rolled out from under the wagon and let fly with a couple of bullets. Ran for the nearest horse and climbed aboard. Didn't look back. Recall some unease about leaving the boy. Fretted over it for a time.

Now, that horse knew this was a make or break moment and he stuck out his neck, lengthened his stride and flew across that plain. Couple of Indians tried to chase me down, but those redskins know when they're beat.

Didn't stop till I reached Flagstaff. The horse, a black stallion with a streak of white lightning down his nose, weren't even lathered. I named him Roscoe. Checked the saddle bags when I climbed down. Threw my head back and laughed out loud when I found them plumb-stuffed to the gills with money. Walked across to a saloon. Ordered a whiskey and then another. Strolled the length and breadth of Flagstaff, till I'd found the best hotel in town. Ate a steak. Took a bath. No mosquitoes.

When a man's pockets are overflowing, a town like Flagstaff can empty them quicker than a sieve holding sand. I'm not ugly. Not exactly handsome. Brown hair. Brown eyes. Five feet and eight inches of average. Once I'd bought me a suit, a hat and a pair of shiny black leather boots, heads began to turn. When I walked in the saloon that first night and paid for drinks all round, my status in town moved up a peg or two.

Certainly became a hit with the ladies. Could take my pick. But a man needs to be careful. Out west, skinny whores ain't skinny due to their eatin' habits. Lay with the wrong one and a man can catch a nasty disease. One that makes his privates shrivel. Didn't want none of that. No siree. Ain't partial to fat whores neither. Never make it to the finishing line, if you get my drift. Don't get me wrong, Lord, I was never pernickety. Red hair. Blonde hair. No hair. Good set of teeth is a bonus but ain't crucial. Way I see it, a man don't look at the mantle when he's stokin' the fire. I had fun. They had fun. Where's the harm, Lord?

Stands to reason what I'd perceived as a fortune was small change to the big hitters in town. Pretty soon, I was checking out of that swanky hotel and taking a room above the hardware store. Wasn't long before I'd pawned my suit and shiny black leather boots for one final deal of the cards. Kept my gun. Ivory-handled revolver, sitting in an open-top holster, butt forward. Man offered to buy Roscoe. Didn't even consider it. Loved my horse. Besides, I had one of those premonitions I'd be needing him.

A queen of clubs and an ace of spades sealed my fate. The two cards I couldn't account for when the game concluded. Weren't in the deck or spread out on the green cloth. They weren't in the winning hand of my opponent. Man was sly and mean lookin'. Wore black. Head to toe. Had friends and associates all round the saloon. Woulda been foolhardy to draw my gun.

I went outside and waited in an alley. He came out alone. Held to the shadows till he drew alongside, then I reeled him in. Pointed my gun at his big fat nose and said, "You stashed two cards, you cheating son of a bitch."

He laughed. Held up his hands, fingers spread. Thought he was being so darn clever till he saw what I could see flashing white in the moonlight. Two cards. A queen of clubs and an ace of spades, poking out from the sleeve of his shirt. I shot him. Took every dollar he owed me and then some. It was time to cut and run. Climbed into the saddle and pointed Roscoe north.

Lord, I aim to be honest and truthful about what I've done in my life, but time is pressin' and it would become mighty repetitive if I related all incidents and events. During those intervening years, I drank, I screwed and I killed more men than was right. Just about covers it.

After the bitter cold of a northern Arizona winter, my wanderings led me south, onto the Farley Ranch, west of Tucson. The rancher's offer of a dollar a day, two hot meals and a bunkhouse to sleep in was sealed with a shake of his hand.

It was roundup time. My roping skills impressed Mr. Farley. Impressed his daughter, Ellie May, too.

Once branding was done, I set to repairing the fences enclosing Farley's territory. It was hot and thirsty work, and most afternoons before I rode back to the ranch, I'd find myself some shade under the branches of a jacaranda tree and take a siesta. One particular afternoon, I opened my eyes to find Ellie May riding up. My Lord, she was pretty. Blonde hair reaching down to a tiny waist. Green eyes. Perfect skin. She climbed down from the saddle and sidled up, hips a-swaying. Sat down beside me, real close. Thighs touching sorta close.

"Thought you might be hungry, Jeremiah. Brought you something to eat."

Now it didn't take long for me to get the idea, what with those flashing eyes and moistened lips, even from the tilt of her head, there was more on offer than a slice of apple pie. I wasn't wrong.

Summer had been and gone when, one day at noon, Mr. Farley wandered into the barn where I was brushing the mud off Roscoe. I glanced up and nodded. For an old guy, he was in good shape. Could make out plenty of hard muscle rippling under his white cotton shirt. Short, fuzzy, grey hair. Old scar tissue filling in the cracks on weathered skin. His arrival made me uneasy. Just stood, chewing on a piece of straw and watchin'. Wasn't my place to begin conversation. Him being the boss an' all. So I carried on brushin'.

"What you doing, Jeremiah."

"Guess I'm brushin' the mud off my horse, sir."

"That's not what I'm asking and you know it."

I looked up. I shrugged. I got back to brushin'.

"Let's do some straight talking, son. You messin' with Ellie May?"

I stopped brushing. He stopped chewing.

"Got a problem with my question, boy?"

"No, Mr. Farley. I like her. And she likes me. Don't see no problem."

He spat the straw out and took a step towards me. I put the brush down and did the same.

"I was gonna run it by you first, sir. Wouldn't be polite if I didn't put you in the picture. You see, I'm planning on marrying Ellie May."

Now I shall never understand why I said that. The

thought hadn't entered my head before Farley's arrival in the barn. Truth was I'd got everything I wanted. Food. A bed with clean sheets. And Ellie May. She cost me nothing and I was content for our arrangement to continue without the need for a gold ring. I guess he'd riled me up and I wanted to see how far I could push.

He fixed me with this cold, hard stare. "Let me tell you something, Jeremiah. You're a piece of shit. I stand in shit all day. Wipe it off my shoes before I go inside my fancy house and eat dinner with my family. And right now, mister, I'm wiping you off my shoes. You've got one hour. One hour to get off my land or I'll put a bullet in your head, cut you up and feed your remains to my hogs."

I met his gaze. I checked out the scar tissue. Noted the busted nose. Ran my eyes up and down his frame and decided I could take him. Didn't need a gun. Didn't need a knife. His old bones weren't equal to his big mouth. Only I'd gone one whole year without messin' up and I ain't a stupid man. I knew Farley was trouble. Big trouble. It was time to cut and run.

You know, Lord, seemed as if Roscoe understood this was the end of the line. He kicked up so much dirt as we galloped off Farley territory, an onlooker would have believed a train had jumped the tracks and was hurtling cross-country.

I rode North. Shot, skinned and ate my share of

marmots and jackrabbits during those years of bedding down under the stars.

Sometimes, when I was skirting a town, with the sun slipping and darkness descending, I'd rein in Roscoe. We'd look down from a ridge onto those pitched-roof framed houses, with lanterns flickering in their windows, and I'd get to pondering. Would picture a scene in my mind. Always the same. Never changed.

I'd have a wife. She was called Rachel. She had blue eyes and wore her long hair plaited, coiled and pinned up round her head. She wore a clean white apron over her frock. She was strong. Handsome. Upright. God fearin'. And she loved me. I was the only man who'd ever remove those pins. I was the only man who knew what lay beneath that frock and apron. And when I walked through the door each evening, Rachel would be waitin' for me.

We'd share a kiss or two and she'd say, 'Time for supper, Jeremiah. Go clean up.'

I'd do as I was bid, and when I returned a pan of stew would be set down in the middle of the table. We'd all sit down and say a prayer and then we'd eat. There'd be a child too. Didn't have a name for the child. Reckoned he'd be a boy.

Liked to dream the dream. Don't rightly understand why. Guess I liked it for what it was. A dream. And dreams don't come true. Not asking for any sympathy, Lord. I chose my own path.

Those days of wanderin' took their toll on me and Roscoe. Decided it was high-time we came in from the wilderness. Crossed the Verde River and headed into Prescott.

Was in a contented frame of mind when I rode into town this morning. My days of killin' and wanderin' were over and I was gonnah straighten myself out. Figured Prescott, with its wide streets and plenty of fancy folks walking on 'em, was the place to do the straightenin'.

Roscoe and I ambled along Gurley Street. Peeled off before we reached the jailhouse. Stopped and touched my hat to a woman in a grey, high-collared frock. Gave me a look from under her black bonnet that could turn milk sour. A whistle and a shriek of laughter diverted my attention to a couple of gals leaning from a window above a saloon. They wore low-necked silk. Their feather boas trailed down the wall towards me. All seemed mighty enticing to a man who ain't had the company of a woman for a long, long time.

Tied Roscoe to a hitching post outside of a saloon on a street named Whiskey Row. Elbowed my way in through the swing doors. Bartender looked up from polishing glasses.

"What can I getcha?"

"Whiskey."

Bartender poured me a glass. I drank it. He poured me another.

"Anything else I can getcha?"

"Feeling kinda' hungry. Could you fix me some food?"

Bartender turned around and hollered. Chinaman appeared from out back. Bartender spoke a few words, Chinaman nodded and vanished to wherever he'd come from.

I handed the bartender three dollars and took a seat in the corner. Back to the wall, facing the door. Old habits. Ran my eye over the gaming tables, the wood-panelled walls covered in steer horns and oil paintings of naked women. Nodded to a couple of old-timers who sat nearby, chewing tobacco and emptying their lungs into brass spittoons. Took another swig of whiskey. Chinaman reappeared. Set down a mug of coffee and a plate loaded with steak 'n' eggs.

I can truthfully say those steak 'n' eggs was the tastiest meal I have ever had. Meat was juicy. Egg yolks ran into the juice. Was mopping up with a chunk of bread when the Chinaman returned.

I handed him fifty cents. "Best meal I've ever tasted. Thank you kindly."

Chinaman was mighty impressed with my tip.

Gabbled away in his own language then put his hands together like he was prayin'. I smiled at him and nodded. Chinaman nodded and bowed. All this noddin' an' bobbin' set me to laughin'. Laughin' so hard, I didn't notice the two men entering the saloon. Had their boots on the brass foot rail 'fore I saw the stars pinned to their lapels. Chinaman saw them too. Picked up the crockery and skooted.

They leaned across to the bartender and said something. Smaller guy, thick set, youngish, kept his hat low an' his eyes directed at the mirror as the taller man turned and looked my way. Had one of those droopy moustaches. Covered the lower part of his face.

I took a few sips of coffee. I pondered on whether my past misdemeanours had followed me into Prescott. But I hadn't seen my face glued to no wall. I finished my coffee, eased back my chair and glanced across. Sheriff and his deputy ignored me. Seemed in deep conversation as I walked to the door and pushed my way through. I took two paces and stepped off the boardwalk, walked round Roscoe and was preparing to climb aboard when I heard the saloon doors swing open.

"That your horse, boy?"

I dropped the reins. Looked around my horse to find the Sheriff with the drooping moustache was standing on the boardwalk above me.

"Sure is," I said.

He took a step toward me. Signalled with a flick of his hand to his badge. "Name's Brown. Sheriff of this town. What's your name, son?"

"Jeremiah."

"Must have cost you some?"

"What?"

"Your horse. How long you had him?"

"Few years. All told about ten." I adjusted the strap of my saddlebag and glanced around. Couldn't see hide nor hair of Brown's deputy.

"You a gambling man, Jeremiah?"

"No, sir."

"So where d'ya get the money to buy the horse?"

I swallowed. Sheriff Brown was asking questions so fast I couldn't think straight.

"Man can hang for stealing a horse, Jeremiah."

We'd been in tight situations before, but I swear I'd never seen Roscoe this troubled. He was fidgeting and twisting, his eyes wild and rollin'. By the time I'd steadied him, Sheriff Brown had drawn his Colt 45 and was aiming to shoot me down.

"Put your hands up."

My hands were going somewhere but they sure as hell weren't going up. As I reached for my gun my horse shied and spun around. Brown took his shot and the bullet, the one with my name on it, drilled into Roscoe's head. My horse gave his life to save me. And it made me mad as hell. I fired my weapon. I shot the Sheriff. I put a bullet into Sheriff Brown's skull, smack between the eyes.

Found the Deputy soon enough. Stepping out from my left, he was raisin' his weapon. My aim was good. Knew I couldn't miss. About to shoot when I saw his face. I saw those big, blue eyes. The same blue eyes of the boy I'd left under a wagon, twenty miles out of Flagstaff, all those years ago. Impact from his Peacemaker sent me staggering into the street.

So here I am, Lord. Light is fading and the blue sky ain't blue anymore. Folks are gathering round to watch me die. There's a gapin' hole where my belly used to be and my blood is gushing and minglin' with the dust and dirt of a street called Whiskey Row.

I, Jeremiah Jones, soon to depart this world ain't seeking redemption. Got only one regret. Should have taken that boy along with me.

Amen.

Watanabe's Honour
Tom Singleton

As cherry blossom falls
So too the warrior
Or his glory is unseen

i.

Watanabe felt the comforting clunk of the undercarriage closing as he pulled gently back on the stick. The aircraft climbed slowly and began a circuit of the airfield.

Kenzo, his mechanic, had told him this aircraft had been on *Akagi* and was one of those which had awoken the giant. Watanabe could believe it. The aircraft was old and stressed and had been in second line training units for some years.

Now, lacking spare parts and fresh oil, its engine had a tendency to overheat. If Watanabe made too much demand on it, trying to climb at full power for example, it would spit oil over the front of the cockpit canopy forcing him to fly almost blind.

Watanabe banked to starboard, turning east towards the bay. The sun appeared to be rising from the crater of Sakurajima as shafts of light pierced the last dark clouds of night and filled the pilot with an emotion he had not known for a long time.

It was not patriotism that he felt as the rising sun filled his eyes but an inner calm and happiness that, this day, his torment of shame and dishonour would end.

Below, other aircraft were taking off and climbing to join him, guided in by the wide yellow stripe painted around the fuselage of his Zero fighter. Watanabe began a second circuit and was pleased to see a green flare rising up from the airfield which was still concealed by shadow. "Good," he thought. "All my little flock are with me."

He glanced in the rear-view mirror that Kenzo had fitted to the Zero's cockpit canopy. Salvaged from an American fighter shot down over the base earlier that week, the mirror increased drag on the Zero but Kenzo had joked that it might save Watanabe's neck. The fact that the last pilot who had looked in it was dead seemed, to Watanabe, to be a favourable omen.

The loose formation behind him comprised an assortment of aircraft types. They were all patched and battered like his Zero, in places its metal skin showing through the peeling olive paint.

Three Aichi Type 99 dive bombers, known as Vals by the Americans, formed a sloppy line abreast, slowed by the drag of their fixed undercarriage. Behind them, but catching up fast, came another battered old Zero fighter. Finally, two big Mitsubishi Type 97 torpedo bombers, called Kates by the allies, brought up the rear.

Watanabe watched them pitching and rolling as their inexperienced pilots fought to control the big, lumbering aircraft.

Watanabe could not talk to his pilots. Radios in Zero fighters were useless and Watanabe had ordered Kenzo to remove them to make the aircraft lighter. The other pilots had orders simply to follow their leader and attack the enemy when they saw him.

With the exception of Watanabe's fighter, all guns had been removed as they were of greater use elsewhere. The method of attack was simply to crash into the biggest enemy ship they could find. Bombs strapped underneath, explosives packed inside and residual fuel were the destructive power of this force. Their motivation was a glorious death and a posthumous double promotion which would bring honour to their families.

Watanabe was to guide them to the combat area and defend them from enemy fighters. This instruction had brought a wry smile to his face.

Denied his request to join the Special Attack Corps because his flying knowledge and combat experience were too valuable to throw away, Watanabe was expected to take on the airpower of the US Pacific

Fleet single-handed to allow the attack to get through. His aircraft, with a drop tank, was the only one with enough fuel to return home.

But returning did not matter to him. Death in battle was all he sought; to cleanse the shame he felt and the dishonour he had brought on his comrades and his family.

The forested hills of Kyushu slipped by beneath them as Watanabe and his flight of crocks climbed slowly and steadily to five thousand feet. From this altitude the land seemed at peace, but hidden was the activity turning the forests into a killing ground.

Bunkers, machine-gun nests and minefields merged with wooden stakes in covered pits and booby-trapped buildings to make a last-ditch defence that would turn Kyushu into the graveyard for a million American soldiers.

A thousand aircraft and one million gallons of aviation fuel were held back for 'special missions', or so Watanabe's commanding officer had told him. With the blessing of Amaterasu, the sun goddess, they would sweep the invader's ships from the sea, as the divine storm had done centuries before.

To his starboard Watanabe could see the distant column of smoke rising from the bombed oil tanks at the Sasebo naval base, north of the great port of Nagasaki. As they crossed the coast and flew south towards the

Ryukyu Islands and Okinawa, Watanabe glanced again in his mirror at the cluster of sad aircraft that followed him.

The other Zero was now ahead of the Vals and on his tail. One of the Kates was tucked in behind the three dive bombers. The second torpedo bomber had dropped behind and lost height, a thin black stream of smoke trailing from its engine like a dirty ribbon.

Watanabe sensed what was about to happen and could not drag his eyes from the plight of the stricken aircraft. Flames erupted from the engine and enveloped the body of the plane which fell like a stone, exploding before it reached the sea.

Watanabe felt nothing for the loss. He had seen much death like that and, on many occasions, had dealt it himself. His happiness turned to serenity as the rising sun continued its climb into the sky. His mind drifted to his past and the events which had delivered him to this point.

ii.

It had been an honour to be chosen, even though his selection was by virtue of the role he had as Lieutenant Akamatsu's wingman. At dawn, six fighters had taken off to escort the Mitsubishi Type 1 bomber carrying the Admiral to the Solomon Islands, on his mission to raise the morale of the men fighting there.

Coming over the sea at fifteen hundred feet they

could see the island, where they were to land, ahead of them.

From the clouds above came the war. Four American fighters, twin-engined P38s, cut in front of them. The lead American inexplicably veered off to port, his wingman following, with four of the Japanese escort in pursuit. Akamatsu and Watanabe remained in position, too far away to intervene, as the two remaining P38s attacked. Horrified, they watched the combat unfold.

The bomber pilot dived, desperate to gain speed to escape the enemy. The guns in the nose of the lead American flashed fire and hits were scored on the bomber's starboard wing.

Watanabe saw the wing fold upwards from the engine and then fall away. The bomber, spinning like a sycamore seed, spiralled into the sea. The American planes were gone and the sky was empty. The six escort fighters landed safely, which was to their everlasting shame.

There could be no greater dishonour than to fail in the mission: to live when the Admiral had died. Even the destruction of one of the American fighters held no salvation. Such dishonour should have been telegraphed around the fleet. Such dishonour should have seen boards of inquiry, disciplinary measures and officers reduced to the ranks. But, in time of war, enemy success is kept a secret so, instead, all six were ordered to die in combat to assuage their shame.

On the day of the disaster, a distraught Watanabe waited outside the tent in which the pilot of a float plane, who had searched for survivors at the scene of the crash, was making his report. As the pilot emerged from the tent, Watanabe approached him.

"Lieutenant," Watanabe said, with as much formality and deference as he could muster for the senior rank, coming to attention and bowing his head."Yes, what do you want?" asked the float plane pilot.

"Did you find them?"

The float plane pilot paused before answering, seeming to realise who his inquisitor was. Watanabe could smell the stench of his own shame. How much stronger must the smell be to others? "All we found was a school of dolphins. Seven of them, one for each man lost." Watanabe stood with his head bowed as the float plane pilot walked away.

In three months, Akamatsu and three of the other escort pilots were dead. Another, Yanagiya, survived because losing an arm made him unfit for combat. Only Watanabe remained unscathed.

He threw himself into battle with reckless abandon. He flew alone at the extreme range of his aircraft to make attacks on enemy airfields. He plunged alone into formations of hostile aircraft. He would fly two or three sorties a day to look for trouble. He remained unscathed and his contribution to the unit's kill tally rose steadily.

The attrition of war removed those who knew of Watanabe's dishonour and he was ordered to take on a fresh pilot as his wingman and pass on his expertise. No longer allowed to fly alone, Watanabe flew again as part of a larger force. But his dishonour remained stuck in his soul and to him the purpose of life was to find death in battle.

Scrambled by the clanging of the empty shell cartridge that was the alarm, Watanabe and eight other fighters climbed high into the sky one afternoon.

Below them were six B17 Flying Fortress bombers, each bristling with heavy calibre machine guns providing a massive weight of defensive fire, as long as their formation was not broken. Watanabe dived towards the enemy aircraft.

The huge bombers filled his gun sight as he closed in on them. He pressed the gun button and closed his eyes. He felt the recoil of his own machine guns and the thump of enemy bullets hitting his aircraft. Then he was through and below the bombers.

One of the big American planes had fallen out of formation with smoke coming from two of its engines. The

Japanese fighters fell upon it like sharks and the bomber was torn to shreds.

Back on the ground Watanabe looked with disbelief at the bullet-riddled wreck of his fighter. It would never fly again. Already the ground crew were stripping it for spares. His wingman approached, elated with his share of a kill and full of admiration for his leader.

"Watanabe-san," said the wingman. "Your *senninbari* has great power. It causes the bullets to pass above your head!" He bowed to show his respect and then left Watanabe beside the bullet-riddled fighter.

That night Watanabe removed his *senninbari*, the thousand-stitch belt. It had been made by his sister and carried a thousand red stitches, each stitch by a different woman: strangers stopped on the street.

Each stitch represented a wish for his good fortune and immunity from harm. In his eyes, it had brought no good fortune but had only prolonged his dishonourable existence. Watanabe wrote a letter to his sister in which he told her only that her gift had been very powerful.

As he wrote he remembered his sister's gentle face. Once she had cried as the blossom fell from the cherry trees.

"Such a waste of beauty," she had sighed.

"If it did not fall it would go unnoticed," was his

father's pragmatic response. He remembered how proud his father had been to see him in the uniform of a naval aviator; Ensign Watanabe. He remembered the tears of his mother falling when he went off to war and he knew then his sister's gift to him had been for his mother.

That night he burned the *senninbari* and scattered the charred remnants on the wind. His loss of honour weighed heavily upon him. Now, surely, he could extinguish the shame that haunted him.

Dawn found Watanabe back to his old habits, in the cockpit of a fighter preparing to sortie alone to find trouble.

He opened the throttle and felt the surge of power pulling from the engine. He waved away the ground crew and released the wheel brakes.

No longer constrained, the Mitsubishi fighter seemed as eager as its pilot to be free of the Earth. Watanabe's aircraft bounced out from the dispersal and taxied towards the compacted sand of the runway.

For a second or two the fighter seemed to hang back, as if gathering to leap. Then, throttle wide open, the Zero roared along the runway, the tail wheel lifting from the ground as it gained speed.

From the darkness of the retreating night came an intruder, an interloper as lonely and as deadly as Watanabe. A P40 Warhawk, with a grinning shark mouth painted around its pointed nose, made one low and deadly pass along the runway as Watanabe lifted into the air.

With no manoeuvring speed, he was an easy target of opportunity. Again, his aircraft was riddled with bullets but this time it caught fire and flopped, rather than crashed, into the waves, breaking on the beach at the end of the runway.

Watanabe was pulled alive from the wreckage. His ankles were broken and his legs badly burned. He had bullet wounds to both arms and splinters had smashed his goggles, blinding his left eye.

He was cared for in the field hospital for a month and then evacuated to Japan where he spent a year in hospital recovering.

Fit for service again, with partial sight in his left eye, he was sent as an instructor to the flying school. There, he gave student pilots (half as good as he had been) half the amount of training that he had received and then sent them to fight the Americans.

In all the time that he was back in Japan he made no attempt to see his family, not wishing to contaminate them with his dishonour and shame.

iii.

Watanabe's thoughts came back to this August morning in 1945 as the sun rose behind them. He glanced again into the rear view mirror and saw the other Zero followed by the three Vals, now in a loose 'V' formation, the centre plane leading.

The big Kate, wallowing and bouncing all over the place, was dropping further behind. With a bright flash, the bomber exploded.

The pressure wave buffeted the other aircraft and a dissipating ball of smoke marked the Kate's last position. Watanabe knew that every last cavity on the bomber had been filled with high explosives, some of it old and highly unstable. The turbulent flight of the Kate must have set it off.

He thought no more about the loss as other worries crowded in on him. "Where are the Americans?" he thought. "They must know we're here."

They had been flying for nearly two hours and Watanabe had expected to see landmarks by now. His view from the cockpit showed only an empty ocean. No ships, no enemy fighters, no islands.

The hole in the instrument panel, where the radio direction-finding compass had been, glared at him like an eye socket in a skull.

The RDF equipment in Watanabe's aircraft had

been taken for use elsewhere long before the transmitter beacon network had been swept away by the war. Watanabe navigated by magnetic compass, hung around his neck on a lanyard, on a fixed heading.

He scanned the ocean looking for any lump of rock he might be able to recognise and get his bearings from. But there was nothing.

He looked at the sun. "Too far east," was his conclusion from its position. Compass error of just two or three degrees had put them miles off course.

Watanabe banked his fighter to starboard, turning to the west. In the mirror he saw the other Zero follow his turn.

The leading Val also followed the turn, taking it through the flight path of the starboard Val which had not turned. Propeller chewed into wing and the first aircraft, still receiving lift from its port wing, flipped over and came to rest on top of the second Val.

Together, like partners in a macabre dance, the two aircraft fell from the sky, exploding only when they hit the sea. The surviving Val, which had made the turn, dived steeply to avoid the collision and disappeared from Watanabe's view. He shook his head in disbelief; four aircraft lost without sight of the enemy. The last Val popped up again on his port wing and Watanabe glared at it. The pilot held up a gloved hand to indicate all was well.

The Val was an old aircraft, designed to operate from aircraft carriers as a dive bomber. Any of these factors could have contributed to structural weakness in the aircraft. This Val was a veteran, relegated to second line duties in 1942. If it had spent the rest of the war doing circuits of a flying school the Val may have survived long enough to be scrapped. But the long flight and the violent evasive action had done for it.

Watanabe held up his hand to acknowledge the other pilot. The Val appeared to shiver and a wave rippled along its fuselage moving forward from the tail. The aircraft's metal skin peeled back and, as Watanabe watched, the tail section buckled and fell off. For a second the aircraft seemed to hang in the air as direction and pitch control were lost. Then, in a vertical dive and spun by the energy of its propeller, the Val fell once again from Watanabe's astonished view, breaking up before it reached the clutching sea.

Practical matters kept Watanabe's mind on the job of flying the Zero. He closed off the horror he had just witnessed as another reality of war. More important was the mission and the fact that he was lost. Then, trouble piled upon trouble. The engine of the Zero misfired and cut out. Watanabe pushed the stick forward, putting the fighter into a shallow dive to retain airspeed. He flicked the switch from auxiliary to main fuel tanks and the engine roared back to life. Watanabe jettisoned the empty drop tank and, free of the encumbrance, the Zero plunged faster into the dive.

At two thousand feet Watanabe pulled out of the dive. The other Zero had followed him down and levelled out on Watanabe's starboard wingtip. Watanabe looked over and was amazed at how close the other aircraft seemed to be. The other pilot slid back the canopy, pushed his goggles up and stared across to Watanabe.

Watanabe looked back into the black, pin prick eyes. He could feel the question carried in the stare. It was a question that Watanabe knew well. It was borne of anxiety but came not from a fear of dying but of dying without glory. A young man, barely twenty years old, alone in an aircraft running low on fuel, seeking reassurance from an ancient of twenty five, who had none to give.

The two fighters flew on side by side. The outline of an island emerged from the haze, still some way ahead. Watanabe looked across at his wingman, waved with the back of his hand and pointed to the island. The other pilot turned his gaze forward and, at that point, his engine stopped.

The three blades of the propeller emerged from their spinning blur, appearing to go into reverse as they slowed to a stop.

The two Zero fighters seemed to hesitate before breaking their formation. Watanabe's fighter pulled ahead. The other, its nose down, began its descent towards the sea. Watanabe watched the fighter, carrying its doomed pilot, fall in a shallow dive until it was too far behind for him to see. He looked in the mirror and saw only the empty sky.

The small island rose out of the sea. Steep and barren, it had topography that Watanabe soon identified on his map. It was one of the outer islands of the Ryukyu chain.

No longer lost, Watanabe flew north, obeying his orders to return if able. Tomorrow or the next day he would fly again. Soon the Americans would come and, without a doubt, he would die fighting them.

The mission had been a disaster. His report would tell how unserviceable the 'special mission' aircraft were. His report would tell how brave men had died for no gain.

Then his dishonour and shame visited him. His report would show that, again, he was still alive when others were dead. His report would deny glory to the pilots he had flown with today; they had not died in battle. Families would receive no honour in return for their sons' deaths. Tears filled Watanabe's eyes.

"We will be heroes," he thought as he banked his aircraft round and headed south again. "Today, we will be heroes. There will be no report."

One ship was all he needed. An aircraft carrier would be ideal but a troop transport would do. One ship, that was all. But, on that August morning, the Americans were not coming by troop ship from Okinawa. Today they were coming by bomber from Tinian and the power of the sun was in its belly.

Out of fuel and alone, Watanabe ditched in the sea. The Zero settled comfortably on the swell. Slowly, as the heavy engine dragged the nose down, water began to rise over the wings and into the cockpit. Watanabe could feel the water around his feet and rising up his legs. He freed himself from the straps that held him in his seat, slid back the canopy and stood up. Tearing off his goggles and flying helmet, in anger and despair he shouted, "Why must I die without honour?"

The sun was high and beat down upon the pilot. Watanabe could see the fins of several large fish cutting through the water some distance away, circling the sinking fighter. "Sharks!" he thought and fear mixed with his shame. He would die as fish food. As they came closer, leaping from the water, turning in the air, Watanabe saw they were not sharks but dolphins, six of them. "One for each man lost," he said to himself.

Watanabe clambered from the cockpit. He stood on the port wing, now awash, and kicked off his flying boots. Then, shedding his one-piece flying suit, Watanabe threw himself into the sea and swam towards the dolphins.

Disney's Dream Debased
Daniel Lewis

I was that mouse: Waving white gloved hands. Fixed smile failing to distract horrified eyes

It wasn't my fault. That's what I'd tell Mark if I met him again. But, as I never will, the best I can do is belatedly offer my side of the story.

*

I left Disneyland shortly after the incident, in June 1984. I was twenty-one, and felt many years older. I remained in Anaheim, California with my parents and failed to achieve a thing, because I couldn't tear my thoughts away from that day. I'd only worked at Disneyland for a year or so, and imagined that disconnecting myself from the 'happiest place on earth' would allow me to forget about Dolly. But, in dreams, I repeatedly saw myself, still pushing the illusion that nothing was wrong.

I eventually landed a job at a gas station in Downtown Anaheim, deliberately opting for the most mind-numbing existence possible. I drifted through life for three years and imagine I'd be there still, staring into the ambitionless void, had I not met Mary.

Maybe I should be thanking Walt, not cursing him;

after all, if I'd never been Mickey, I'd have struggled to start a conversation. But, as Mary dumped Oreos and water on the counter and paid for her gas that day, I asked what I always asked the pretty girls.

"On your way to Disneyland?"

"How'd you guess?" she replied, brushing stray blonde hairs behind her ear.

I shrugged. "Call it intuition."

"You been?"

"I used to work there."

A smile. "Very cool."

I never expected to see her again but, a few days later, she returned. Bought Oreos and water, no gas.

"Disneyland was amazing, as usual," she sighed. "What did you do there?"

"I was a cast member," I said.

"A *what?*"

"A cast member. That's what they call their staff, especially the ones who wear costumes."

"And did you?"

I handed her her change, our fingers touched. "What?"

"Wear a costume?"

For the first time in months I allowed myself to remember, her expectant smile and too-blue eyes keeping me calm.

"Sure," I said. "I was Mickey Mouse."

She nodded. "My favourite. And who are you now?"

I extended my hand. "Tom."

A man joined the queue behind her. She ignored him as she took my hand. "Wouldn't Jerry be more appropriate?"

"Not really," I laughed, confident that the past was willing to let me go. "I'm no longer a mouse."

Finally, at the age of twenty-four, Dolly dissolved away and I realised I could somehow make amends and become a better man. Or, simply, become a man.

Within two years, we'd left Anaheim. Mary hated everything about the city, apart from Disneyland; I just resented my memories, and believed that leaving the area was the only way I'd ever truly move on. We settled in Garden Grove; hardly a huge leap from Anaheim, but far enough away to convince us both that we were embarking on a new life.

And it was a new life. Garden Grove was the most beautiful place in Orange County I'd been to. Neither of us were religious, but the Crystal Cathedral was a breathtaking sight and, overall, Garden Grove was smaller, more diverse, than Anaheim could ever be. We felt immediately at home there, and I loved the idea of living somewhere not defined by cartoon characters.

I married Mary in 1990, around the time I realised I

wasn't cut out for nursing. I'd tried for almost a year to make a difference, but just didn't have the stomach for it. So I embarked on a teacher training course, then landed a job at Bolsa Grande High School, teaching literature; the one subject I cared about as a student.

*

I've done well. I have a steady job, a wonderful wife and three children I adore. Yet what amazes me is that, all these years later, the most impressive thing about me is that I once worked at Disneyland. My Garden Grove friends love the fact that I was once their favourite mouse. More importantly, my kids couldn't be prouder; I am, to them, the personification of all that is joyful, thanks to my time working for Walt. At seventeen and fourteen, Zack and Sarah are too old to still delight in my mouse tales, but Abby is six and believes that her daddy once had the greatest job known to humankind. She loves watching Disney films with me, and can't sit through one without asking if I once knew her favourite characters. I don't like to let her down, so tell her in Mickey's shy, falsetto voice: "But of course, Abby."

Fantasia is her current favourite. Or, rather, 'The Sorcerer's Apprentice' segment. You know, the one where I cause all manner of chaos.

My children, my wife, my friends: they all see my past as a magical experience. And why wouldn't they? I only ever told my parents and a handful of Anaheim friends about what I was a part of on 3rd January, 1984, and thankfully they never mention it.

I could've told Mary about the incident. But I wanted her to be my future, my new start, and didn't believe that'd be possible with my crime hanging over us both. Sure, she finds it strange when I opt out of trips back to Disneyland with the kids, but when I tell her the place makes me too emotional, she leaves me be.

It's better this way. I want the kids to believe Disneyland is as magical and pure as Mary still assumes it is, that life is as wonderful as Donald and Goofy insist it can be. I don't want them to ever picture their own Mickey Mouse, sitting on a bench in the staff changing rooms, white gloved hands too numbed to remove his tear-stained mask.

And, because no one in Garden Grove knows my story, it no longer exists.

Or, rather, it didn't until recently.

Now, the truth's come careering towards me, I'm crying myself to sleep every night, and it's all Mark E. Smith's fault.

*

I was a punk kid, into Dead Kennedys and other Californian hardcore bands, but I'd mellowed slightly by the time I joined Disneyland. Just as well, given their no-

nonsense attitude towards dress code; I don't think they'd have approved of my spiked hair phase.

Once at the gas station, my tastes broadened. I befriended Danny, a music obsessive seven years older than me, doomed never to graduate from gas pumps. He introduced me to The Velvet Underground, The Stooges, Sonic Youth. Then, once he was sure I was ready, he let me loose on The Fall.

I had – have – never heard a band like The Fall. They formed in 1977, I think, so many miles away in Manchester, England, and yet sounded…counter-exotic. Their post-punk tag didn't do them justice; they were abrasive, lo-fi, driven by repetitive riffs. And, at their centre, stood their only constant: Mark E. Smith, barely singing his way through the splendour; effortlessly witty, sometimes obscure, always poetic. He was, and still is, the ultimate frontman, happy to fire one or all of his band at the slightest whim. They're still going, over thirty years and nearly thirty albums later, but they're less a part of my life than they once were. And yet we are connected. We've been connected for twenty-five years and, until recently, I didn't have a clue.

Danny didn't appreciate it when Mark E. Smith's then-wife, Brix, joined the band; maybe that's why he didn't recommend the first album where her presence is really felt: 1984's *The Wonderful and Frightening World of*

The Fall. So I never got round to buying it until a few weeks ago, when I found a cheap vinyl copy on eBay and decided to give it a go for old times' sake.

I'm glad I did…or, at least, I was; it's poppier than earlier efforts, yet still peppered with noise and oddness. The last song is my favourite. Atypical of The Fall, it's a melodic, disarmingly gentle tune…Not that you'd guess so from the title.

'Disney's Dream Debased'.

As soon as I scanned the sleeve for the song's name, I felt uneasy, and questioned whether its subject matter was as bright and breezy as its tune suggested. I listened to it repeatedly. I found the lyrics online to make sense of Mark's near-unintelligible vocals, and then, as a long-forgotten queasiness once again rose within me, I did my research and discovered what I already feared.

They say you shouldn't meet your heroes.

Well, I met Mark E. Smith years ago and never knew.

I wish I still didn't know, because his presence changes everything.

He was there, and he wrote a song about the worst day of my life.

*

Dolly Regene Young, a grocery clerk from nearby Fremont, visited our 'happy place' on Tuesday, 3rd

January, 1984 with five friends from Tempe, Arizona. She was forty-eight years old, but I don't know to this day if she was married or had kids.

I'd only been at Disneyland a few months and was having a ball. Loads of people my age to work and – after hours – get wasted with. Many Minnie Mouses to flirt with. The job was exhausting, but working with people I liked made it worthwhile. My best friend there was Alan, also twenty-one, but with two years' more Disney experience. For over a year he'd worked as Goofy, until he swore at some kid who mistook him for Pluto; he was then relieved of his costume and set to work on the Matterhorn.

One of Disneyland's main attractions, the Matterhorn is a rollercoaster ride modelled on the mountain in the Swiss Alps. I imagine Dolly and her friends would have been excited to experience it, sitting one behind another in their bobsled, impatient for the fun to start.

I didn't work on the Matterhorn, but was located nearby. After only a few months on the job, my smiley demeanour and rapport-building skills had got me noticed, and I'd been rewarded with the cast member role everyone wanted: Mickey Mouse.

It took a while to get used to the costume, even though I was Disney's ideal height and weight. The heavy rubber head caused my neck and shoulders to ache, and the thick costume gave me heat rashes. But these were problems any cast member faced, and rendered insignificant by the joy the job brought me, the joy I effortlessly bestowed on others with a nimble dance. Everyone wanted to be seen with the mouse, kids and adults alike. They believed in me. Most days were taken up simply posing with guests, my perfect round ears, wondrous eyes and lovable smile brightening up endless photos. I was the embodiment of happiness, of childhood dreams made real. If I took your hand in mine, your Disneyland visit was complete.

And, at around 3 p.m. that day, as I made children giggle and adults blush, way above me on a make-believe snow-capped mountain, Dolly Regene Young was thrown at speed from the rear car of her bobsled onto the Matterhorn's tracks. She landed on her back, then struggled to her feet as an oncoming sled smashed into her at twenty-eight miles per hour. Dragged briefly along on this second, unexpected ride, Dolly died from horrific head and chest injuries. When the bobsled stopped, her body was mangled and meshed within wheels, forevermore a part of the Matterhorn.

I didn't see her die, but I heard the screams made by her friends, by our guests, by adults and children who never thought they'd witness such sights at Disneyland.

I didn't see her die, and neither did Mark. But,

according to an old interview I found online, both he and Brix had been on the Matterhorn only ten minutes earlier. Brix said Dolly had been decapitated, which wasn't the case – that would have been a preferable sight – but her recollection was otherwise accurate, including her description of-

Well, of me. Of my actions.

As soon as people realised there'd been a fatality, they ran to their favourite cartoon characters for solace. The accident was speedily reported by one of the cast members – Dopey, I believe – and, within minutes, paramedics were on the scene. The Matterhorn ride was shut down, and the surviving guests were briskly evacuated via an elevator hidden within the mountain. Meanwhile, me and Br'er Bear, Dopey and Pluto and all the other poor bastards dry-retching into oversized masks, had to somehow remain calm, restore order and draw attention away from the blood on the tracks, the flesh all around, the ripped clothes and matted hair of Dolly Regene Young.

At Disney University, cast members are trained to never say "I don't know". They must answer all questions or call for assistance. And it's impossible to describe why but, when you're in that uniform, you…conform. Keep the illusion alive. We were taught to put on a good show and ensure everyone remained happy. But we were never prepared for this.

I don't recall anyone approaching me who resembled Mark and Brix; I simply remember indistinguishable faces, panicking as I was panicking, expecting Mickey Mouse to make everything alright. Faced with a crisis I was never trained to tackle, head full of inane regulations, I was bombarded with questions I didn't know the answers to. It therefore seemed easier to stay in character and distract distraught guests from the sight of paramedics, of the police making their cautious appearance.

Though, as a cast member, I was not supposed to speak to the guests, I raised my arms and appealed for calm. I don't know what I said, only that they were words of comfort, for some reason uttered in my trademark falsetto. And, as my humpback whale shoes shuffled closer to the scene, as I saw glimpses of tragedy and cold efficiency, my mouth gaped in horror and my eyes watered. But Mark and Brix, grandfathers and daughters, teens and infants, never saw my reaction. They saw my mask: big eyes suddenly mocking, wide smile now malevolent. Saw my white gloves wave, my coattails flap, my too-big head tilt from side to side as I made believe all was well. Saw Disney itself turn macabre, as the mouse jumped with joy at the sight of blood, hair and tissue.

I'm there, in Brix's interview: not a real animal and

yet barely human, laughing in Mark's face as he near breaks down in tears. And I'm there in his song: now flapping at Brix, a minor but unwittingly sinister part of the horror he conveys.

A real life atrocity cartoon, immortalised in song.

*

Eventually the audience dispersed. Mark left Disneyland, I imagine, gripping his wife's hand tighter than usual. I made my way to the scene, as paramedics separated Dolly from her final ride. I think she was slim with brunette hair but, really, I'm guessing. I think I saw a cracked pair of glasses resting by an undamaged leg but, again, I'm not sure. All I know is there was blood and confusion and a sense that more than a life had been lost.

They removed her body. Police and officials replaced Br'er, Pluto, Dopey and me, and moved stragglers on. Maybe if those in charge had stepped away from Dolly's death, from the bad publicity it threatened, they'd have realised that their staff were in as a bad a way as their beloved guests. But no one asked me if I was alright. Why would they? I was grimacing wide, as usual.

I retreated backstage to clear my head and my stomach, then returned to work, pushing Disney's now-soiled dream. I recall walking around, Alan by my side, neither of us squeaking a word. Post-Goofy, Alan had become one of many responsible for checking seatbelts before the Matterhorn ride commenced and, as we hazily walked in circles, it was obvious that Dolly's death had disturbed him.

The following day, the story was widely reported around Anaheim. Disneyland spokeswoman Laura Dike confirmed what had taken place, but the focus was wrong: instead of talking of tragedy, the papers reminded us that the park had welcomed over 230 million guests in twenty-eight years. When pushing such big numbers, the mention of Dolly becoming only the seventh Disney fatality made her sound like part of an impressively low statistic. Equal emphasis was put on Detective David Tuttle's assertion that Dolly's seatbelt was open when he examined the bobsled, despite assurances from a park spokesman that all the airplane-style belts were secured before the ride began.

So did Dolly's belt malfunction? Or did she undo it herself? And, if so, because it needed loosening? Or because she no longer wanted to be constrained, because she had dark thoughts her friends from Tempe, Arizona could not know about, because she wanted to end her fake-smile existence as grimly as she'd lived it?

For weeks, such questions clouded me. I struggled to breathe behind my mask, and was soon advised to step out of my costume and work on a food stall. But it didn't matter what I was tasked with; I couldn't focus. I'd lost my spark, my Disneyfied cheer, and knew I had to get out.

Once I started work at the gas station, I felt calmer, yet somehow less of a man. Perhaps Alan felt the same; within a year, he was found outside some Anaheim bar, overdosed and in full Goofy uniform. There was no evidence to suggest that his decision was connected to Dolly's death.

Soon after I met Mary, I read that Dolly's family had settled out of court. Richard E. McCain, Disney's attorney, said discussions had been "fruitful"…and that was the last I ever heard of the case. Whether her family knew they couldn't beat such a sweet-smiling foe, or were simply offered enough to back down, I'll never know.

All I knew back then was that it was time to let Dolly Regene Young – and Mickey – finally rest in peace.

*

But 'Mickey Mouse' is also a slang term, applied to something of dubious quality.

For almost twenty-five years, I managed to force Dolly's death from my mind. But now, thanks to that song, the past has come slamming back into me at twenty-eight murderous miles per hour. Mark E. Smith has shown me that, despite my life in leafy Garden Grove, despite my loving wife, three fine kids and a career to be proud of, I am a Mickey Mouse human being, forevermore debased.

'Disney's Dream Debased' is the most important song I've ever heard and I can never hear it again.

There are tears in my eyes as I place everything I own by The Fall in a large cardboard box. It's not enough that *The Wonderful and Frightening World of The Fall* goes; it has to slide alongside the other thirteen albums I've amassed over the years. I can no longer bear to hear Mark E. Smith's voice. It doesn't matter whether he's singing about hip priests or his new house; all I hear is his contempt for me.

*

I keep my promise to Abby. I wake her up Saturday morning, feed her some Cheerios, and take her with me to the music exchange store. I imagine she has some ulterior motive for asking to join me, but it seems she just wants to spend time with her daddy. Understandable, I suppose; I haven't paid her much attention lately.

She watches in silence as the shop assistant seizes my box, barely registers the quality of the vinyl inside, and hands me fewer dollars than the albums are worth.

"I like being with you, Daddy," she says as we make our way home.

Suddenly aware that I am free to forget my past, my voice cracks as I reply, "Same here, gorgeous."

"Daddy?" She hesitates, then asks, "When we get home, can we watch *Fantasia* together?"

I almost say no. But I look at her beautiful too-blue eyes, wide with belief in a place where happiness resides, and nod with a cartoonish smile. I prepare for my next performance and realise I will never move on. Never truly leave Anaheim or that song behind, and never begin again.

I am, and will forever be, that mouse.

Our Song
Marc Nash

He pelted down the grassy knoll at full tilt. He didn't stop until he ran slap bang into the car door. The serrated squelch of flesh stopping up hard against glass reverberated in the still air. Head splayed against the passenger window, legs pinioned against the steel door like a butterfly mounted on a cork. If she didn't know him better, she'd believe him to have had the very life crushed out of him. But she knew him very well indeed. It simply wasn't possible to know another discrete human being better than they knew one another. He was doing his outsized-bug-squished-against-a-metal-carapace routine. Again.

She herself took more dainty steps down to the knoll, since it was icy underfoot. As it unfailingly was at this frozen time. The frore grass crinkled as she tiptoed along, a sound that conferred shivers down her spine which owed nothing to the temperature. Lovers' Lane always had that effect.

She arrived at her mate spreadeagled against the unyielding barrier. She canted her neck just enough to see that he had interposed his hands between his temple and the glass. Skilful sleight of hand, consonant with him being a wrestling devotee, where all along you knew the violence was artfully implied. The two of them hadn't implied or faked anything, however.

Finally he bobbed his head. His hands now serving for blinkers, as he tried to pierce the darkness within. He arched his shoulders back in order to unclamp his pate from the window. Affording his breath some range to wreathe itself against the glass. Then he rubbed at it with the elbow of his puffa jacket. He returned to his scrutiny, moving his hands around the window like a doctor tapping a chest cavity. He shot her a grin, then blew breath out towards her, yet it never arrived. Freezing and petrified in the air before being able to lick her with a burning raw kiss. "It's on the inside, alright." She contented herself with a tight nod and concentrated on working her chin deeper into her coat's muffler. "Same as it ever was" as he rapped on the window. His knuckles were covered in rime.

She walked over to the driver's side. She gave it a cursory glance, before she too blew on the window and then rubbed away at it. Her woollen coat didn't emit the same nerve-shredding friction squelch as had his puffa. She wrapped her hands around her shoulders and tried to hug herself warm. Nothing doing. He shifted over to the side of the bonnet, bevelled both fists down on to it and stared into the space between his arms, as if consulting an imaginary map. Or trying to remember the co-ordinates of some blurred memory. She was burrowing deeper and deeper into herself. He couldn't catch her eyes. He extended his hands across the bonnet's partition out towards her. She didn't break her obtection, the pupa yet to bloom into a butterfly. He wiggled his fingers. He would unthaw her. He always did.

She tried not to break into a smile, but she couldn't steel herself enough. She branched out her arms to meet his hands. Palm to palm, his dwarfing hers. They brought the pads of their fingers together, steepling their fingers. He quickly manoeuvred them to interlock and, before she knew it, he had raised them into a vault over the bonnet. She knew what this was a signal for. They both started sidling along their respective sides of the car, hands joined in a wedding arch, canopying the car beneath them. On reaching the boot, back they turned once again. Picking up the ceilidh's pace, moving into a skip. Wheeling this way and then that, rocking their arms as their exertion trails hung in the air like unspoken sweet nothings. Like confetti frozen in mid-flight.

They collapse across the bonnet. Steam rising from both of their bodies chafed at by the cold air. Great beaming grins on their empty faces. He winks at her. They slide off the bonnet and resume their vaulted arch.

Two grooves diverging from the slick ice on the bonnet mark their wakes. As they dance, they bring their arms scything down over the bonnet and boot and raise them back up to clear the bubble roof. This time they do not keep to their side of the car, but carry wildly on round the chassis, dipping their heads into their respective front seat side windows. Seems they are possessed of enough boundless spirit to keep this reel going for eternity.

*

The hand, pinned between a shoulder and passenger seat, has developed pins and needles. Colloquially termed 'going to sleep', when in fact it is feverishly pounding its pain gong to rouse the rest of the body which is in slumber. The tiny stabs initially are absorbed into a persecutory dream, but somehow the overwrought brain manages to convey the internecine nature of these forces and stir the boy into consciousness. He can't believe they've fallen asleep, tonight of all nights. He tries to extricate his hand from its press. "Mmm, don't. I'm comfortable," she murmurs. Using his free hand he contents himself with picking away a curl that has fallen across her closed eye. She curls up closer into his puffa padded warmth, still in the land of nod. He takes the opportunity to recover his hand. It feels swollen, though he knows this only to be the interruption of the blood flow yielding untrustworthy impressions for his grey matter. He holds it against the quilted weave of his other sleeve. It is hard to determine which of the two is more inflated right now.

He fumbles with the key in the ignition. The problem is he can't calibrate his movements with a hand that's not only awry, but also shaking. He grabs its wrist with his good hand and steadies himself. He manages to turn the key. "What, so soon?" she inquires dreamily. "No, I'm just trying to warm you up." "Cos I'm not ready-" "No, it's okay. I'm not ready, either. Nothing's connected up." "Oww, oww, oww, it's blowing cold air, you wally!" "Sorry. The engine needs to warm up first." "It's not worth it. And I was having a lovely-" She looks up at him, panic in her eyes. He smiles gently and dabs once again at her recalcitrant fringe with reassuring fingers. "No. It doesn't really matter, does it?" He entreats his lips to hold their smile, but cannot see that they betray him by blanching themselves of honourable colour. But in the crepuscule she fails to regard this and, besides, she is engaged in wiping sleep from her eyes.

"It's okay to feel a little bit scared." Some part of her yearns to raise her head from his shoulder and confront him, but its leaden heaviness only yields torpor. "How can you tell?" His smile widens into a genuine grin, that crooked grin he knows she is unerringly smitten by. "You're trembling!" "Well I'm freezing, aren't I?" "I can feel your heart pounding, too!" He mimes the motion of her ticker, breasting his hand against the skin above her heart, then veering it sharply away with the systole. Neither are aware that it more approximates the action of cardiopulmonary resuscitation. She snakes her hand out and rests it on his jacket. "I can't feel your heart through your coat. Shows how thin mine is." He arches his shoulders back and makes as if to shuck them from his coat. "We can swap if you like. I'll wear yours." "Don't be daft. It's too small for you. It'll rip at the seams." "So what? What difference will it make?" She tilts her head to look up into his face, pressed back into the headrest since he is still frozen half-in and half-out of his jacket. Her face appears to have dropped ten years of ageing, to a time just before he knew her. To a time when she would most definitely be regarded as a little girl. But now, such part-regression back in time, when still planted atop a young woman's body...God, she is beautiful, even when drained of her usual sparkle. He wonders what his face reveals of him right now. He decompresses his upper body back into his jacket.

"I'm so tired. I want to get it right, you know? Is this what it will be like?" This is an impossible question to answer, but he feels some response is called for. His whole upper body naturally puckers towards a shrug, but he manages to depute his fingers to stroke her cheek.

She recoils under his touch. "I'm very scared. Hold me." "I'll never let you go." Finally, she lifts her head and lasers her eyes on to his as surely as were she tugging his chin with her fingers into direct alignment. "How do we know? How can you say that for certain?" He has to hold her gaze or the moment, the lifetime, will pass for ever. He can't even allow himself to blink. Can he risk holding her shoulders to demonstrate his resolve? "Cos we love one another and nothing can change that. Absolutely nothing." They hold each other's stares, looking for a chink. Praying to be steeled in the forge of their eternal love, to have the impurities of thought burned off. His fingers span her cheeks and he pulls her into a kiss. Searing and unfamiliar in the freezing air, even the sound rasps beyond wonted flesh on flesh. Her lips quavering. Holding steady he soothes her tremors. She blinks her eyes shut. Fancying he can discern what's expressed beneath the closed lids, he exhales softly. The breath should have gently stirred the shutters over her eyes, ruffling them open as was the norm. But it's sideswiped and beaten down by the chill.

"Give me your hand." She blindly gropes a hand to fumble into the open-cupped embrace of his. "No, no. You need to open your eyes for this." She complies, more from weariness than either irritation or curiosity. Still holding her hand, he leans away from her towards his driver's side window. He breathes on it and brings her hand up to the fogged patch. He uncurls her index finger and uses it to incise through the condensation. He etches a heart from the opacity. Then he extends a finger of his own and draws a second, interlocking heart on the window. He appends their initials and considers an arrow. But by now the breath has evaporated, returning the window to its single translucency. "Very symbolic," she snorts, dragon vapour trails of breath emitting from her nostrils. "We've disappeared in the blink of an eye." He smiles and leans once again to gently exhale over the area. Their hearts, of course, rematerialise. He keeps up his conjuration by breath over several waxes and wanings. She stares fixedly at both the empty void and the recurring proclamation of their love. "That's all well and good, but it will only last until they tow the car away, scrub it down for clues and then crush it." "No, they'll give it back to my parents. And don't forget the mix CD. That will have to get them to see." He reaches inside her coat and pulls out a caseless CD. It's silver sheen seems alien in the gloom.

"Shall I put it on?" She bites her lip but doesn't respond. "'Heroes'" starts palpating the speakers. "I've been thinking about the music-" "Bit late to make any changes now." "No, not the track listing. But how do we know which song will be in prime position?" "What do you mean?" She has turned away from him, scrolling breath on to the passenger side window. Her gnawed nail trails its wake, but he notices that her finger is shaking. Is she trying to convince herself, as she executes her own twin hearts to posterity? "I mean, which track will be playing when we finally drop off the charts? Which will be the ferryman's song?" "Who knows? It will be on continuous play. Bit like Russian Roul-" "Until the car battery gives out. Then it will all go dead and they won't know." "Who cares? Just as long as we know which song is the last to ring in our ears?" "But this is all about providing definite answers for them. Making it so unutterably clear to them that they are hopelessly wrong about us. There can't be any loose ends. As sure as eggs are eggs, they're going to turn everything over and look for any inkling." "Look, it will be obvious. Short of us doing it with a samurai sword and daubing a message in our blood on the lounge wall-" "Don't! Just don't. This is hard enough."

  He moves in to hug her silent. He dips his head and bevels it into her abdomen. It does seem to take the fight out of her. Or maybe just her breath, tugged and wrenched from her by the wincing cold. "Are we sure this method is going to work? Not the aftermath, I mean the actual journey itself?" "It's foolproof. It's probably the most common method." "Well how come, even with the heater on, it's so damn cold in here? That must mean the air from outside is getting in somehow? That the car's not properly sealed?" "It's fine, I promise you." "Then what about where the hose comes in? It won't be a perfect fit and enough air might get in to spoil things. We could end up vegetables. Alive but cut off from one another." "I'm not feeding the hose in through any windows. I'll hook it up so that the warm air blowing through the heater here will deliver us the exhaust fumes." "Exhausted fumes." "What?" "Nothing."

She hits the track button and returns the disc to the beginning. He has a flashback image, normally when she's leaning forward like that, to reapply her lipstick using the driver's mirror. He's usually the one tasked with the soundtrack for any stationary passage in the car. He looks at the dashboard's clock. It will be light soon, he thinks to himself. "If we don't do it soon, someone might see us," he offers flatly. "It's still too early. Who else would be up at this time?" "Well us, for one." "Apart from us?" "I dunno, doggers maybe." "Don't! You always have to cheapen it, don't you?" "I'm sorry, babes. I'm sorry. I'm so sorr-"

*

They cease their dance, once again facing their respective side windows of the car. He raps his knuckles on the driver's, his fist precisely in the centre of the love hearts. He receives a thumbs up from inside. He drops her hands and walks slowly over to the rear of the car. A rubber hose lies limp and forlorn under the chassis. He sinks to his haunches and has to prop himself up against the car to prevent himself overbalancing. His hand is trembling, but he manages to thread it over the rusty exhaust pipe. Corroded or not, the metal chastises his flesh with an icy touch. He steps awkwardly out of his crouch and trudges back to the driver's door. He knocks on the glass once again, but this time with less percussion. The engine revs once, but then settles back into its contented purr. Evidently it is having no truck with the cold affecting its performance.

She pops her head up over the roof towards him. "Which one is playing now, can you hear?" He places his ear against the glass, but it is shaken free by the car's vibration. "It's hard to tell. It's all a bit fuzzy. That might be the gas dampening everything. See, told you there was no problem with it being sealed." "Oh yes, you were so right about everything." She holds out her fingers and waggles them at him. Whether her intent was to mock, he gives no indication of being affronted, but merely grasps them. They massage each other's fingers while entwined. "You didn't stay with me!" He yanks both her arms towards him, forcing her chin on to the bonnet. "You went first, leaving me on my own. Looking at you and not being able to have you." He swivels her wrists in his, twisting and contorting her arms, elbows pointing outwards like question marks. "Well, you'd already let go of my hand. More concerned with your own throat than us going together." She strains to reverse her upturned hands, but he holds fast. Her wrists exposed from their sleeves appear vulnerable. The veins enticing and goading. "It was an instinct. Nothing I could control. Your throat constricts..." He drags her forwards, wholly on to the bonnet. With its slick rime, she slides right up underneath his face. He looks like he could either slap or kiss her. "Yeah well I must have gone first 'cos of lower body mass or something. The monoxide overpowered me faster." He distends his arms and sends her skidding back across the bonnet away from him. He brings one hand up to his throat, she still fully extended at the end of the other hand. "Things we never thought of. Could never have thought of." Still gripping his hand, she works up on to her haunches and slides back across the bonnet, scissoring her legs a straddle round his hips. "The body puts up a hell of a fight. But our love overcame it all the same." He wheels away so her body whips round away from the car. He starts rotating on the spot, spinning her round the fulcrum of his body. They wheel around ceaselessly, until alerted by the car's engine cutting out. "Stop! It's making me dizzy. I feel...light-headed."

He gently levers her back to the ground. She

dismounts from him. They each return to their respective sides of the car. He grasps the door handle, but is careful to buttress his body against the panel. He only wants to inch the door ajar. The door clicks open with a sodden clunk. He slithers his hand in to prop up the boy inside. He gapes the door further open. The boy's body sags towards him, but he is able to brace the slump. He repositions the corpse upright. Then he reaches across it to gently cup the girl's head turned away against its window. He gets his hand beneath her cheek and gingers her head away from the window. Her matted hair erases the faint imprint of the interlocked hearts. He places her head so that it is sitting on the boy's shoulder. He leans across, down into the footwell. He fumbles sightlessly around the floor until he is able to grasp the coarse stem. He brings the rose up and interlaces it between her fingers. He slowly extracts his hand as he backs away from the open door. He is outside the car once again. As he places the flat of his hand against the edge of the door, his face is parallel to the driver's window. He realises that the initials within the boy's hearts have not been reversed, in order to broadcast to the outside world. Little matter, he shrugs, since the hearts are barely discernible within the glazed smudge condensed by the gas. "I remembered to do mine, though," she chastises over his shoulder, having come round to his side of the car. She leans her face on his shoulder, her chin nestling on the bone in order to peer beyond. He does not protest the driving pain.

"Ah, the afterglow." "They do look pleased with themselves." "Positively radiant." "Angelic cheeks of the innocent." "Of course! What have they got to feel guilty about?" "Don't start that again." "Do you think they're dreaming of each other?" "No, I think their sleep is dreamless." "And eternal." "And eternal, yes. Except for the anniversary. When we turn over to avoid the coffin sores." "We were just two young kids, really." "Exhausted kids." "Exhausted kids indeed. Up way past their bedtime." She jabs her chin into him to vacate. She slams the door shut. Unseen inside, the two corpses flop away from another again with the impact of the door wresting them apart. The rose drops into the footwell.

Personal Study
Jacky Cowper

The car kicked as Paula forced it into first and eased it into the street.

She spotted David around about the same time as he saw her. He raised a hand to wave, and smiled. Three of his mates were lurking around with him. They half turned their backs as she pulled up beside them.

David nodded a muted "bye" to his mates and stubbed his cigarette out on the brickwork behind him. "Gotta go..." he laughed, and with one easy movement hoisted himself into the open-top Ka.

She gunned the engine, listening to the whoops of the guys, and pushed out into the steady traffic. Her blonde hair caught in the breeze and played gently around her shoulders.

He took a strand of it in his hand and twisted it round his fingers. "Where are we going for lunch, then?"

She concentrated on the dashboard and the traffic, checking the rear view mirror regularly until they left the narrow street far behind. "We could have some sandwiches at my place for a change."

He withdrew his hand, then cautiously replaced it

on her shoulders.

"Will there be pot?"

"There could be."

"Then sandwiches sound good."

She briefly pushed her neck against his hand, then drew her own hand across the front of his shirt, pushing the tie to the side. His body was slim, hard, toned. His free hand reached over and slid her fingers through the gap between his buttons. She forced herself to pull free and grip the wheel again, guiding the car expertly through the traffic.

"How far?" David asked. "I can stretch to an hour and a half, but after that I'll be missed. And I'm getting very peckish…"

Five minutes later, they were pulling in to a reserved space outside a block of newly built flats in the west of the city.

David again left the car without using the door.

Showing off, she reckoned, but she swirled her keys and he fell into line just behind her, like a faithful puppy.

Her flat was modern. There was little furniture but he liked it. The walls were pale, perhaps magnolia, and the surrounds were white. It looked clean, functional but homely. He decided that he could live here, and settled onto the settee. Paula was in the compact kitchen. He could hear the clink of glasses. She called out to him, "Red or white?"

He wasn't sure. "White, I think."

"Great," she answered. "The pot is in the jar by the TV. Help yourself to a joint. Don't be greedy, though. We both have to get back to work this afternoon."

"Cool," he said, and had a look for the biggest one he could find. He spotted the matches in a long glass dish by the side of the gas fire and lit one. He drew the perfumed smoke down into his lungs, held it for as long as he could, then exhaled, too quickly, and ended the moment with a racking cough.

"Shit, this is good...shit!" he gasped.

Paula swung through from the kitchen, her hips sleek in a silky robe.

"Wow!" he said, taking the glass of wine and handing her the joint. "Fuck me!"

"Oh, I intend to," she said, and snaked her free arm round his waist. She smiled as she felt the smooth skin under her palm. "Get undressed."

He tore his jacket off and was about to undo his tie when she stopped him. "Keep the tie, I like it." She took both ends of it and pulled him towards her. "It could come in useful." Then, before he could protest, she began to kiss him: his face, his body. She felt her nipples harden.

He wasn't sure how he got out of his shirt with her

hand still gripping his tie, but he managed. It fell in a crisp, white heap onto the pale brown carpet.

Her hand tore at his fly buttons. He took another suck at the heady dope. His head began to swim; he laughed. He could feel himself stiffening as she slid her hand round the back of his buttocks and pulled his body towards her.

He grabbed her hair in his free hand and thrust her head towards his groin. Sensing his thoughts, she pushed him onto the settee and, as he flapped, trying to regain some balance, she went down on him, stroking him with her tongue, fondling him with practised fingers until she could feel he was almost ready.

He groaned with pleasure and tried to hold her head down, but she moved his hands off her and slid onto him, clenching and holding to maximise her pleasure.

As they came, she yelled and collapsed forward onto him. He was laughing now and holding her body, touching her breasts carefully and slowly, until she was moaning and purring beside him.

"Shit, that was good…well, everything," he gasped.

"Oh yeah," she said, and nuzzled the small curls behind his ears. "And we've still got forty minutes left before I have to get you back."

He glanced at his wristwatch. She was right.

The joint was nearly gone. "Can I have more?

Pretty please?" he asked, holding up the stump.

"No," she said. "It's too strong. You'd be caught. But have some more wine. I hate opening a bottle and not finishing it."

He drank the cold wine. He realised he was still nearly naked, and pulled a fluffy cushion over himself to cover the remnants of his erection.

"Have you got any music?" he asked, looking for a diversion so he could pull his trousers back up.

"Of course. What do you think I am? Some ancient old bag who doesn't know her Red Hot Chili Peppers from her Coldplay?"

"Coldplay. They're a bit lame." He saw her face drop. "Of course, I quite like them."

He reckoned he'd covered that one quite well…

She searched through her CD collection until she found the one she wanted. He watched as she slipped the CD into the Bose player. Her feet were flattish and she had a bunion coming at the base of her big toes. He'd read that wearing high heels for too long could do that to a woman's feet, but he hadn't seen it before. The slight misshape fascinated him, and he found he was barely listening to Coldplay as 'Violet Hill' washed through the apartment.

"What else have you got there?" He walked across the carpet, pressed himself against her and stroked her rump through the silk.

Before she could stop him he'd reached past her, his long arm snaking over her shoulder towards the case.

"Blondie," he read. "Depeche Mode. Who the fuck is that?" He couldn't help laughing at the weird names. He wasn't even sure if he was saying them right.

She pushed him away and poured the last of the wine into his glass.

"It doesn't matter," she said. "Why not just listen to the fucking music?"

He got the distinct impression he'd messed up. He grabbed for her arm, but she pulled free and slammed the door to the hall behind her.

"Come on!" he yelled at the door. "I was just kidding. I know them. They did that one about the aeroplane, the one that dropped the bomb on Hiroshima. Noel Gray. That one."

He slumped onto the couch and drank more of the wine. It didn't taste so nasty now. Maybe he should get dressed. He retrieved his shirt from the floor, slipped off his tie and pulled the shirt over his shoulders. His left shoulder blade was itchy today. He'd need to get some of that cream for the spots again. He tucked the shirt in as he fastened the trousers and put the tie round his neck. He tried three times to do the Windsor knot before he gave up. It had always given him issues and now, with the plonk and the pot, the simple task was well beyond him. He looked around the flat once more, taking in the photographs for the first time.

He wandered over to the unit where they stood and peered at the smiling faces.

A girl of about nine looked back at him, her smile gappy. Her hair was the same unmistakable shade of blonde. A boy, about fourteen years old, smiled beside her. His hair was dark.

Must have taken after his Dad, David thought. Wonder where they are now?

The door to the room was opening. He jumped back over to the couch.

She came in, fully dressed.

Her face was puffy and her make-up slightly blurred.

"I'm sorry," she said. "I overreacted."

"I'm sorry, too," he said, leaning over and wiping a tiny clump of mascara from her cheek. It made a small black streak along her skin.

She smiled up at him. "And by the way, you ass, it was Enola Gay, not whatever you said."

They giggled together and sat back down on the settee.

"I guess we don't have any more time left." He looked at his watch. "I really have to be going."

"I know," she said. "But we had a good time, didn't we?"

"Sure did," he replied. "But I need to get back."

"Don't keep saying that," she replied, irritated. "You're like a broken record."

"Vinyl," he said. "It's vinyl now."

"If you carry on like this you can walk back." She grabbed her coat off the back of the door. "Get your jacket on."

He picked it off the back of the chair and brushed a long hair off the crest on the pocket.

"Aren't you going to fasten your tie?" She noticed the ends swinging against his shirt.

"Can't," he mumbled, and hung his head. "My mum usually does it for me."

"You cretin." She grabbed him, pulling him towards her, tugging the material into the required shape. She patted it once it was done.

They walked out of the flat into the stairwell, her heels clicking on the shiny stone, and made their way down the stairs and back to the little red car.

This time David waited until she'd put the key in the lock and opened the door before sliding into the passenger side and fastening the seat belt.

She drove without speaking, her face harder in the glare of the sun. She squinted, trying to see. He saw lines and maybe even some wrinkles he hadn't noticed before.

"Under the dash, there – my dark glasses."

He took them out of their case and handed them to her.

She snapped them on. "You kids," she said. "You're all the same. Hot bodies, teasing all the time. Looking for action. And when you get action you don't know what to do with it. Asses."

The words peppered him like grape shot. He shifted uncomfortably in the chair, unsure what the correct comeback would be.

She pulled up at the wide iron gates. This time there was no one about. Classes were in.

"Well, thanks, I guess." He looked over at the school hoping he wouldn't be seen. So far he'd only missed personal study, but maths started in ten minutes and his absence would be noticed. After that was a break, and his mates would be keen to get all the gory details. Sure she was a bit older than he'd prefer – but hey.

She waited until he was standing on the pavement again, his hands in his pockets as he scuffed his foot against the kerb.

She kept the engine turning over in case a warden appeared. She was idling on the zig-zags after all.

She looked at him. He was a fine looking kid,

maybe sixteen. Maybe not. In a couple of years' time he'd be a great catch.

She'd been harsh. She needed to let him know she was still available. He'd been a great ride, after all.

"The pleasure was all mine," she said. "But if you wait for me again tomorrow, maybe we'll take it a little slower."

He nodded and turned towards the gates. She watched until he slipped inside the glass doors before driving away.

"First love," she said to no one in particular. "What a bitch."

The Other Side
Lee Williams

This room is small. A security office in a stately home like Beesley Grange needn't be much larger, particularly outside the tourist season (May to October, Open Sundays for Guided Tours throughout the Winter Period). Still, it is cheerful enough in its own way, although furnished in a fairly spartan style. There is a desk, a computer, a bank of screens showing views from the cameras, and a small pedal bin. On the wall is a calendar (November is represented by a cat dressed as Marilyn Monroe), a clock (it is just after midnight) and a newspaper clipping with the headline 'HERO SECURITY GUARD SAVES YOUNG BOY FROM GANG'.

  Three of the walls of the room hold doorways and the fourth, directly behind the desk, is almost entirely taken up by a window which crackles with the incoming rain. The three doors lead variously to the corridor which links the Eastern Wing of the house with the Grand Staircase; to a tiny kitchen with a sink, kettle and microwave; and to a windowless toilet colourfully decorated with a selection of nudes ripped from specialist magazines. On the back of the door to the corridor hang a raincoat and a long scarf.

The clock is ticking.

A young man is sitting at the desk, dressed in a black jumper, black trousers and black tie. His name is Thomas Perkins and he is generally addressed, within this room at least, as Perky. His hair is fair and unkempt, but an onlooker's attention would be drawn first to his face. It is difficult to describe his face.

His attention is fixed on an object in his lap. For security guards, it is essential to have a hobby which is largely silent and solitary, and can be concealed swiftly beneath the desk when necessary. Electronic games are popular choices, as is masturbation, but Thomas' favourite has always been reading. He finds that concentrating his attention on a book seems to mitigate the static which has plagued him ever since the attack, the terrible hiss which blends with the rain and runs all his nights into one another. When he reads, he feels as if a clear pool forms in the centre of his brain, pushing the static outwards where it clogs his ears and crackles in his hairline, but leaves him free to think and dream.

This evening, he is reading an old leather-bound book, the journal of Sir Henry Beesley, filched from the bookshelves in the Master Bedroom. He has read this book every night for almost three months, over and over.

The currently visible page reads as follows:

Saturday 17th March, 1917

The blister growing in the corner of Uncle Percy's portrait broke open today, discharging a great number of tiny spiders which trickled away down the woodwork and across the skirting boards. Spent the best part of the day capturing them and releasing them into the gardens. The most curious thing is that they all bore some small resemblance to Uncle P himself. More comical than sinister, really. Some walking with his old limp, others whistling snatches of his favourite music-hall numbers in tinny voices. A few even sported his elaborate moustachios!

Could it be that the dead only forget their earthly ways gradually, just as a body decomposes? That they mix into the greater ghost over time? Perhaps there is a field in Flanders which bristles with a phantom like a great forest, among which there yet exist traces-

It's certainly an unusual sort of diary, and a flick through its yellowed pages would reveal many other similar entries (in fact, they are of an increasingly fantastic bent from 1916 until the final entry in February 1918), but this alone does not explain why Thomas reads it so regularly and raptly, or why his fingertips seem charged with a delicate electricity as he turns the pages. Thomas feels a deep connection with this book.

When he first found it three months ago, he had been troubled for some time by a number of visions which he had assumed were a consequence of the attack. Aside from the emotional trauma of those long hours in the garage, he knew that the injuries to his head could also have caused a more physical sort of brain damage, whatever the hospital said. So he had told no-one when he began to see ghosts.

Besides, who would he have confided in? His fellow security guards? His poor nocturnal mother? Intelligent and sensitive boys from the working class learn at an early age to walk softly and carry a big bushel, and Thomas had taken this lesson to heart. So he held his peace, never telling anyone of the gurning faces which strained from the woodwork of old doors, or the poor stunted souls which toddled through the guest bedrooms in the dead of night, quacking like ducks.

It helped that there seemed to be no malice in the apparitions. They did not appear to be aware of his presence; did not, in fact, appear to be aware of anything. They came and went at random, babbling and squeaking, passing through and into one another, marbling the house with their presence. They sweated from the damp patches in the attic and pranced in crazy shapes through the geometry of the wallpaper, or churned together joyfully in the Italian Fountain. Sometimes he recognised a face from a painting or sculpture, but he found it difficult to comprehend that he was seeing dead people until the day he realised that he wasn't. After all, if something is dead then surely it is gone from the world, but these ghosts (as he now thought of them) clearly hadn't gone anywhere. If they had, then how could he hear them rattling through the pipes or see them nodding and shivering in the tree-tops? They had simply changed, and they continued to change.

Only one ghost ever seemed to have kept any semblance of an individual person, or to have any awareness of its surroundings, and that was the ghost which sometimes appeared in the Library. It only sat, and waited, and went again.

The clock is ticking. Thomas draws in a deep breath through his nose and picks gently backwards through the pages of the journal. He stops when he comes to this entry:

Thursday 16th July, 1914

Richard stopped by today in his new motor car. Marvellous engine, quite terrifying to think of him haring around the countryside in it. Jack and Dolly were with him and a pretty little thing called Charlotte or Carole – some such C name. Couldn't help but feel a little glow of the old fatherly when I saw the way she looked at him. How he does it I'll never know - I don't recall having the same effect in my heyday! Still, those were different times, and I did eventually win the ham, as I used to tease her by saying. Only wish she could be here now to see her boy all grown up.

I must say, Jack has turned into quite the-

Thomas is smiling wistfully as he reads this. He has never had a girlfriend himself, is unlikely ever to have one now that his face and his confidence have been shattered. His teenage dreams used to swell and purr with female flesh like tropical hothouses, but since the attack he is more likely to have nightmares. Sleep brings him only a fever of knives, sneers and indignities, endlessly replayed.

He sometimes permits himself to flirt on the telephone with Jenny from head office, although he has never met her in person. Outside of business hours, calls are redirected to the security room where he notes down any bookings for guided tours and relays them to her at the end of his shift, just when she is arriving at work.

Often he will tease her by making up a booking of his own.

"I've got one here for an A. Baba plus forty," he will say, or "Do we have space for an S. White plus seven?"

"You're awful!" she says when she catches on. Her voice is lovely, soft and reassuring. He tries not to allow himself to picture her face.

One of the monitors flashes erratically and Thomas peers up at it. A mess of shapes swarms through the Eastern corridor, disrupting the transmission. The static fizzes louder, swamping his brain. He knows the tapes won't have recorded any of this. The most the other guards ever experience of the ghosts is a slight interference with their radio signals or a displacing of the letters in their text messages.

To clear his head, Thomas stands and opens the window. Leaning out, he lights a cigarette and inhales deeply. He holds out one of his palms against the rain as it comes in horizontal from the moors, letting it prickle sharply against his skin like the tiny teeth of a puppy.

Behind him, the wind takes a page from the journal where it lies on the desk and turns it with gentle reverence. Then another, then more, until it rests open on this entry:

Sunday November 11th, 1917

More and more nights I sit in the Library and sometimes he comes and sometimes he doesn't. I always know it's him because there is a red smudge about his neck, the scarf his dear mother knitted for him. Those moments are the only things I cling to, but are they enough? They make things bearable, I suppose, but I begin to envy the phantoms now. They seem unaware of everything, unaware of each other like the crowds in Oxford Street. I can't go up to the City any more. They say they don't need me but the truth is it's easier for them if I'm not there.

Why does he not seem so lost as the others? What is his purpose? No matter. It is enough to feel that one has some connection left in this rotten world. My darling son-

    Thomas closes the window and returns to the desk. He sits down and stiffens when he sees the pages of the journal have turned. Leaning over to read the new entry, he lays a finger gently upon it.

    The phone rings. Thomas picks up the receiver.

    "Hello, Beesley Grange. How may I help you?…Oh, hello mate. What's the matter?…I see…Yeah, it's this weather, isn't it?…Okay mate, I'll hang on until you get here…Yeah, I'll do one more patrol then put my feet up…See you in a bit."

He hangs up, then writes in the logbook:

00:23 - Guard 116 telephoned to say he will be half an hour late in arriving for his shift due to car trouble necessitating a bus journey. Guard 121 agreed to extend his shift.

Thomas sits back and frowns slightly. He is looking at the newspaper clipping on the wall. 'HERO SECURITY GUARD SAVES YOUNG BOY FROM GANG'. When they came back a week later and dragged him into that garage he didn't feel like a hero, nor did he when he found himself in hospital with his face all bandaged up. He doesn't feel like a hero now. A hero probably wouldn't lie awake wishing he hadn't got involved, or feel his insides flip over every time he hears a group of teenagers laughing.

What Thomas doesn't realise - what his lack of self-esteem won't allow him to admit - is that he would do it again if he had to, and he would take the consequences again.

He turns the pages of the journal carefully, to and fro, until he comes to the entry he is looking for:

Tuesday May 1st, 1917

I saw him! He has come home somehow, as I knew he would. Fought his way back from the mud of that awful place. The presence I have felt in the Library for the last few weeks must have been him. Last night he materialised faintly just for a minute, just long enough to let me know he was there, that a part of him had survived. Knew it was him, even though his poor face was ruined, just as Jack described. I cried when I saw him but no words would come. Said them all later to his picture. How proud I was of him, of all those brave boys. My beautiful son, I shall wait for him every night.

Thomas closes his eyes. The static presses in on him, sealing him completely. Outside, he knows, the Ghost of Beesley Grange churns joyously around him, mixing past and present together, burning off the bitterness of old lives. Beyond that, the weekending town surges with drunken abandon, and beyond that, stretching all ways in space and time, warring and copulating with itself, is the world. Fizzing in the darkness. A host of lights, never dying.

It is enough, Thomas thinks, to make a connection. He writes in the logbook:

00:35 – Guard 121 commences final patrol of interior.

Then he picks up his torch and radio, winds the long red scarf about his neck, and sets off for the Library, as he does every night.

A Life In The Day
Lev Parikian

Detective Inspector George Carden shifted in his seat and allowed a bubble of wind to escape from his bottom. A glazed expression passed fleetingly over his face as he felt the gas penetrate the torn upholstery beneath his massive buttocks. He gathered his thoughts, scratched his left nipple, and turned his attention to the young constable standing before him.

He really does look like a cow, he thought.

"And what can I do for you, young Henderson? More trouble with library vans?"

There had been an incident the week before, and much mockery since. Henderson was not taking it well.

The lad blushed.

"No, sir. Nothing like that. Actually, sir…we…that is, Kite and I…we wondered if you could give us a helping hand with a case."

"Fire away, young Henderson. Fire away."

"Well sir, there's this suicide…"

Carden looked up.

"Go on."

"Man blew his brains out at a set of traffic lights."

"Witnesses?"

"A traffic warden, sir. She…"

"Shagged a traffic warden once," interjected Carden. "Name of Rita. Lovely lass."

Henderson was clearly nonplussed by this unwarranted reminiscence. It occurred to Carden that the thought of sex with a traffic warden may well not be on the young man's radar. Must be getting old, he thought. Policemen look like foetuses, and I wouldn't touch a traffic warden with a bargepole.

"You do realise, Henderson, that suicide isn't, per se, a crime? And that this is, if I'm not very much mistaken, the *Criminal* Investigation Department?"

"Well, sir. There's curious circumstances."

Carden leaned back in his chair and slapped his desk with the palms of both hands.

"Ah, now then. Curious, eh? By a strange coincidence that's exactly how I like my circumstances, Henderson. And you're hoping that my decades of experience and legendary acumen will help shed light on said curiousness?"

P.C. Henderson's reply was as bland as an air sandwich.

"Yes, sir. Something like that."

"Perhaps you can elucidate further, Henderson."

"Sorry, sir?"

"Elaborate. Illuminate. Explain. Tell me what the fuck's going on."

"Oh. Right. Well, sir, we've established his identity. He had his wallet on him."

"It's astute deduction like that that gives the force a good name, Henderson. Well done."

"And we've been to his place of abode."

"Proceeded, Henderson. You proceeded. Must get your jargon in order."

Henderson's blank look told him all he needed to know.

"Never mind, lad. Never mind."

The kids that joined the force these days. You had to feel sorry for them, really.

"We are fast approaching the moment, Henderson, when you tell me exactly why you are involving me in all this."

"Sir, I think you should come and have a look for yourself. It's what we found at the house."

Carden groaned to himself. His carefully planned afternoon of indolence was rapidly going tits up. Retirement, still six months away, couldn't come quick enough.

He heaved his pendulous frame out of the chair. The whole room seemed to quiver.

"Lead on, Henderson. Lead on."

*

Had Henderson been more experienced, he might have described the suicide's place of abode as situated at a mile and a quarter's distance from the police station, in a West-South-Westerly direction. Carden preferred to say it was just round the corner from his favourite chippy. He stopped there to avail himself of a bag and joined the young constable a couple of minutes later in front of the large semi-detached house that had been the suicide's final home. It would have been nice, once, but decay now oozed out of every crack in the render and Carden felt his spirits plummeting even lower as he crossed the weed-ridden front drive.

"Chip?"

"No thanks, sir. Trying to keep the weight down."

"The curse of youth, Henderson. Get to my age and you'll be past caring," replied Carden, shovelling chips into his mouth. "What do we know about him?"

"Richard Ward. Twenty-eight. Ex-military. Decommissioned three years ago. Unemployed since then. Landlady says that he k…"

"Kept himself to himself and didn't talk much."

Henderson looked a bit surprised but carried on, reading from his notebook.

"There are eight rooms in the house, five of them currently occupied. We haven't had a chance to speak to all the other tenants yet. Kite's busy with the counting."

Carden felt the first stirrings of interest.

"Counting?"

"Come round the back of the house, sir," said Henderson, glowing a bit.

He led the way through the shadows to the side of the house, past the bins, and into the garden.

Carden stopped and stared. He immediately saw what Kite was counting.

Holes.

The garden had been dug up. It was large, about a hundred foot by fifty, but instead of lawn, Carden found himself looking down on innumerable little holes. Each one could have been no more than six inches wide and the same depth, and there was a tidy little mound of earth next to each one.

"Henderson, I want you to contact all the garden centres in the area and ask if they've had any suspicious orders for three thousand crocus bulbs. Kite!"

Constable Kite was at the other end of the garden, standing under a large fir tree, his head bowed in concentration. He held up his hand.

"…Three thousand nine hundred an' forty-five…hold on…three thousand nine hundred an' forty-six…be with you in a minute, sir…three thousand nine hundred an' forty-seven…just a few more to go…three thousand nine hundred and..."

Carden interrupted him with a jovial bellow.

"Eighty-three, nineteen, seventy-twelve-and-three-quarters, two hundred and twenty-six thousand three hundred and eighty-eight..."

Kite gave him as reproachful a look as he dared.

"I'll have to start again now, sir. And I was nearly done."

"Never mind that, lad. Let's just call it four thousand, shall we? I shan't tell if you don't, eh?"

And he gave the young man a heavy, conspiratorial wink.

Kite was a sallow-faced young man whose angular features contrasted comically with Henderson's bovinity. He looked hurt by Carden's imputation of relaxed morals.

"I would like it to be exact, sir, in case it has some bearing on the case."

"I don't give a bin bag full of mongoose gonads about the bearing on the case. Let's call it four thousand and be done with it."

Kite stood there, uncertain as to what he was supposed to do now.

Poor sods, thought Carden, looking from one bewildered junior to the other. They don't know what they're doing or why they're doing it. They're saddled with me as a boss, and they don't know what I'm going to do next. Better go easy on them for a bit.

He stood for a second, surveying the scene. The holes formed an asymmetric pattern across the garden, but there was no doubting the care with which they had been dug.

No, bollocks to it, he thought. They've got to learn sometime.

"Must have taken ages. Don't you think, Henderson? Ages to dig four thousand holes. And he's done it carefully, too. Look at the tidiness of it. Don't suppose anyone saw him doing it. Or maybe they did, just thought it was a bit strange. How long, do you think?"

"Sir?"

"How long to dig four thousand holes this painstakingly? Even if you're doing one a minute, that's three days' digging, if you don't stop. He'll have been out here for weeks, won't he?"

He looked up at the stern facade of the rear of the house.

"So those rooms are the unoccupied ones?"

"She said the ones at the front are more popular."

"And nobody comes out here in January, do they? So nobody will have seen him doing this because the garden isn't overlooked by anything else. Hope you're following all of this, Henderson. Advanced detection techniques. Otherwise known as talking to yourself."

Henderson was silent.

"More to the point, why?" continued Carden. "That's the main thing. That's what Sherlock bloody Holmes would be asking. Why?"

"Don't know, sir."

"But then, Henderson, we don't actually need to know why, do we? The criminal part of this investigation is very straightforward. In fact, there is no criminal part, as I said at the outset. The poor bugger's done himself in in front of reliable witnesses - nobody more reliable than a traffic warden - so there's no question of foul play. We've no need to do any more than that. Simple case, really. I shouldn't be wasting time and resources on it. But I have an itch, Henderson. When a young man kills himself I want to know why. And I particularly want to know why he's dug up his back garden beforehand. I want to know if it's part of something bigger, or whether he was just another victim of his own and the state's inadequacies. Especially when said young man has seen active service, like this one. Because it seems to me, Henderson, that there but for the grace of God goes every one of us. You, me and Constable Wouldn't-Know-Shit-From-Shaving-Foam Kite over there."

Carden threw the empty chip bag to the ground and wiped his greasy hands on the back of his trousers. Henderson dipped down and picked up the bag.

"I'll just put this in the bin, sir, if you don't mind. Don't want to be litter bugs, do we?"

Carden turned towards the young constable, an unaccustomed intensity rising in his jowly features. It looked for a second as if he was going to grab Henderson by the lapels. He spoke with a hint of menace.

"I retire later this year, Henderson. And I can tell you one thing for free."

"Sir?"

"Nobody, but nobody, is going to be saying 'That George Carden, he were a terrible copper, but you know what? He picked up his litter.'"

"Yes, sir."

"Now give me that bloody chip bag."

He turned on his heel and strode purposefully out of the garden, depositing the bag in one of the bins on his way. He called to Henderson over his shoulder.

"Let's go and have a look at this room, Henderson. We're not going to learn anything else here."

"What about Kite, sir?"

Carden turned. Kite had started counting the holes again.

"Fuck me," muttered Carden, "he's got about as much sense as a fuckwit smoothie. Kite!"

Kite looked up.

"I thought we said four thousand. Now come with

us. We're going detecting."

*

Twenty minutes later, the three men stood in the late Richard Ward's room. They had searched it thoroughly and found precious little to give any clues about anything, but the sparse furnishings, filthy windows and overbearing smell of stale marijuana smoke told their own story.

Carden manoeuvred himself into the only chair. Under his weight it resembled nothing more than a rickety assemblage of cocktail sticks held together with dental floss. It groaned under the barrage of human flesh. Then, after a few seconds, it bowed to the inevitable and collapsed, depositing Carden onto the floor.

"You're not even thinking of laughing, and that's an order," he said. And then, when no reply or help was forthcoming from the silently sniggering constables: "Come on, help me up. It'll take me half an hour by myself."

They hauled him to his feet with some difficulty, and surveyed the wreckage of the late and alleged chair. Amongst the debris was a small black notebook.

"Aha!" said Carden. "It would appear, gentlemen, that we are not the crack investigative unit we thought we were. Pick that up, please, Kite. Don't fancy scrabbling round down there again quite so soon."

Kite bent down to pick up the book and handed it to

Carden. He leafed through it, frowning.

"This is going to take a while. His writing's terrible. Looks like an ant with a nosebleed's walked across the page."

He tucked the notebook in his jacket pocket.

"Back to the station for a cuppa, lads. We're on the trail."

*

Monday

More dreams. They get worse.

I went to the meeting today. The doctor was nice. He said it might help if I wrote things down. Don't know if it will help but will see.

Tuesday

I don't know how I can do this.

Saturday

Wake up. Fall out of bed. Comb. Head. Cup of tea. Or coffee. Can't remember now.

I have to rush out because I'm late, but I don't know what for. There is nothing for me to go to except the doctor's appointment, and that was yesterday. He asked me again if I was writing things down. I said I couldn't. And I can't talk. It will not change a thing.

They chucked me off the bus. I was just having a

smoke. But that's not allowed now. Nothing's allowed now.

I can think of nothing but limbs. They fill my dreams. And I dream all the time, even when I'm awake. The girl's leg landing beside me.

I can't get a job. I have no money. This place is a shithole but it's all I can afford. All the money I have goes up in smoke.

The doctor says I need to write it down which will help. But how? And how does it help the girl?

Monday

Wake up. Fall out of bed. Comb head. Cup. Late. Bus. It's all the same. Every day. In every way. The smoking makes it a very little better. I can escape just a very little bit.

Tuesday (I think)

This can't go on.

Thursday

I saw the doctor yesterday. He seemed happier with my progress. I said that yes so was I. He said that I seemed to have gone through a barrier. I said that yes I had. He said that I seemed lighter. I said that yes I was. He asked if I was writing things down. I said yes I was. He asked if it helped. I said yes it did. It was a lie, but it seemed to make him happier.

Actually, writing it down does help. Things are clearer now. I know now that I have no choice. It's nobody's fault. It just can't go on like this.

A landmine is an evil thing. Our job was to clear them. It takes hours to clear just one. First the detector, then the slow digging away, then the detonation. It takes ages. And you have to get them all. The thing about a landmine is that you don't know where it is until you tread on it. And that's what the girl did. We had been through the whole field. We really had. But it turned out we hadn't.

It just takes one.

No matter how long I dig, I can't find it. But it's there. I know it's there. It just won't be me who finds it.

Sorry.

*

Carden pinched the bridge of his nose and looked up at the two young men. Henderson thought he looked exhausted all of a sudden.

"So that's that, then. Nothing complicated. No deep abiding mystery. Just a man broken by things over which he had no control."

"Very sad, sir," said Henderson.

Carden looked at him with something approaching contempt, made as if to speak, then thought better of it.

"Yes. Very sad. That's about the size of it. Very sad."

"Is everything okay, sir? You seem...different. Quiet."

Carden sat slumped in his chair. No, lad, he wanted to say, I'm no different. I've always been like this, but I've never let you see it before.

But he decided against it. Instead he rummaged in his ear with his finger, picked out a small ball of wax, and rolled it thoughtfully between finger and thumb.

"No such luck, Henderson. Just another day. Now where's that bloody cuppa?"

The Taffeta Wall
Carole Pitt

Christmas had been less than joyful. Heavy snow and freezing temperatures had gripped most of the country for over two weeks. None of our kids had been able to make it home, which meant I had plenty of time to worry.

My old van laboured on the snow-covered track and slid to a halt outside my sister's house. Her bedroom curtains were closed, so I decided it would be foolish to disturb her hangover. I didn't blame her sleeping in, considering the present situation. I was amazed I'd got out of bed. Self-discipline is a hard thing to curb sometimes. I made it back to the main road and, with a metaphorical black crow firmly anchored to the top of my head, I drove slowly to the workshop.

The old mill house had an interesting history. It had once been a splendid residence for a cloth merchant in the 18th century, but now it was like any other industrial complex, shabby from the persistent carving up into various-sized units. My neighbours ranged from car-part dealers to a guy who made the most magnificent stained glass. There were varying degrees of success amongst the current tenants. Some were doing very well but others, like me, were feeling the effects of the financial crisis. Number 4a's front door still bore the graffiti my son had sprayed during his last year at university. I opened it and found a stack of mail. During the last month the volume had steadily increased, mostly reminders of previous bills. I gathered them up and climbed the worn stairs to the first floor.

My rule was never to open any letters until after a strong coffee. I drank the first cup too quickly then looked around. We had closed three days before Christmas and not bothered clearing up. Neither of us could muster much enthusiasm. It wasn't as if we had customers queuing up outside for our services. On this, the first Monday of a new year, I viewed the mess with indifference. I opened the envelope from the bank, the contents of which politely invited me to pay off my overdraft by the following week. To delay acknowledging it I placed it face down by the sugar bowl and noticed a few mouse droppings on the surface. As I rarely used sugar, I wasn't bothered.

An empty feeling hung over the place. The three women machinists who had worked part-time for over five years were gone. Their overalls were still hanging on the coat pegs, a reminder of the good days before the credit crunch. Even the sewing machines had an air of neglect, and I began calculating what they were worth for resale.

There were eight industrial machines altogether. Five flat beds, two overlockers and a blind hemmer. The latter I was still paying for. Even if I could sell them for half their original cost, it would never cover the loan and the overdraft.

I trudged up to the second floor, the cutting-out room. Nothing of any value caught my eye, other than a very large fire extinguisher and a few rolls of fabric gathering cobwebs. A fire on the premises had never worried me, but thinking about the potentially combustible material I allowed myself to fantasise. It would be a way out of a difficult situation, as long as I was prepared to spend a few years in the nick.

The trouble was that freedom from any difficult situation usually comes at a price. I started sweeping the floor and tried plotting another way out of the mire. Twenty minutes later I heard the unmistakable clump of Flo's boots on the stairs.

"Sorry I'm late, I had a bad night," she said.

"Nothing unusual, then," I replied.

"I thought you'd be round early so I didn't set my alarm. It's freezing in here; shall I put the heating on?"

"I'd have a look at this first," I said offering her the bank's communiqué.

"Can I take a couple of paracetamol and make the coffee first?"

"Try not to break the habit of a lifetime, especially when I'm facing financial ruin."

"I forgot to tell you Sandra's popping round soon," Flo said, handing me a cup and ignoring my jibe.

Flo's old school friend was a pain in the backside. I hadn't seen her for a few months and the prospect of a visit didn't improve my mood. Sandra enjoyed the sound of her own voice too much.

"Don't encourage her to stay long. She does my head in."

"There's something important she wants us to know," Flo said.

"Well we've heard that one before," I said, but I was curious. "Any idea what it is?"

Flo emptied the mice-infested sugar bowl into the waste bin; she was going to do the unthinkable and tidy up before her friend arrived.

"She always wanted to live in Australia, so maybe she's come to say goodbye. I'll miss her if she does."

"She'll save money on the tanning parlours," I offered.

Sitting drinking coffee and delaying the showdown with the bank manager was making me nervous, and bad nerves affected my eyesight.

"Have you seen my goggles?" I shouted.

"I haven't. Get a chain and hang them round your

neck. I'm sick of reminding you."

We were heading towards one of our trivial arguments, but the appeal to keep it going wasn't there.

"Leave the tidying. If you want something to do before Sandra gets here, the hem on Mrs. Carver's ball gown needs finishing."

At least the alteration service hadn't suffered a complete melt-down: it was boring and repetitive work but I was in no position to turn it away.

Flo looked a bit pale and I suddenly felt guilty about my attitude. I took a couple of deep breaths and tried to calm down before she got upset. I gave her a reassuring squeeze and went off on shaky legs to make the dreaded call.

The long conversation resulted in a temporary reprieve. The upshot was if I could pay off the overdraft by the end of the month the bank would not call in the loan. I rubbed my hand across the dusty window, experiencing a rush of relief. There had been difficult times before and we'd always managed, but I'd vowed if things didn't work this time I would pack up for good. At least Flo had her teaching qualification; if she practised getting up in the morning she might find another job.

A silver Jaguar came down the drive and parked in our property owner's space. A blonde woman got out and waved at the two lads who ran the card company; they were spreading sand on the icy road. Just as well; the woman began teetering in our direction on three-inch stiletto heels. Sandra had arrived. I decided to be hospitable and went downstairs to greet our guest.

Sandra Blackwell was a striking woman in her early forties and she looked remarkably improved since our last meeting. She seemed more polished and certainly better dressed. The fur coat wasn't a fake and I didn't offer to take it from her because the workshop hadn't warmed up sufficiently to cast aside a three quarter-length mink. While Flo got busy washing cups, I opened a box of chocolate biscuits, a present from the car parts people.

"It is nice to see you girls again, happy Christmas," Sandra said, producing two shiny carrier bags containing bottles.

"That will cheer us up," said Flo, giving her a hug and taking possession of the gift.

"You both look a bit miserable. I hope nothing's wrong," Sandra whispered.

Flo was about to launch into an explanation of our troubles, so I lifted my hand in warning. I didn't want her washing our dirty laundry in public.

We sat down and made small talk for a while, the usual gossip. Other people's sleeping arrangements, the latest divorces, any other scandals, etcetera.

"What was the important news you wanted to tell

us?" Flo asked.

Sandra pulled her mink coat around her and blushed.

"I'm pregnant, ten weeks approximately."

I could see Flo was stunned, and to be honest so was I. Of all the scenarios Sandra would have been likely to come up with, pregnant wasn't the one I'd have guessed. According to what I had heard, she hadn't wanted children. Age must have mellowed her. We both offered our heartfelt congratulations and meant it. I knew this wasn't the end of the story, so I sat and waited. Sandra didn't disappoint me.

"There is something else I'd like to discuss with you," she said regally. "Because of my condition, I'm getting married sooner than planned and I wondered if you girls can make me a frock?"

"How soon is soon?" I asked, wondering if I could add extra to the bill for the pressure involved.

"Three weeks. I've tried several places and there's nowhere that can do it in time. They all say my design is much too complicated. The bridesmaid's dresses are taken care of so no need to worry about that. Judy, you are my last hope, I know you and Flo won't let me down. I have to have this dress, so I'm begging you."

It seemed ironic; we were struggling to survive, but here was a customer practically on her knees. Gauging how much she'd be prepared to pay was tricky; I didn't want Sandra to think we were desperate. Flo had a bit of a sparkle in her eyes; just the idea of cutting out yards of bridal fabric had bucked her up.

"Have you got a design in mind?" I asked.

Sandra reached for a big leather bag. She opened it and took out a plastic folder.

"The theme for the wedding is Henry the Eighth, so the dress, I think, is called Tudor-style."

I took the A4 sheets of paper and began looking through them. Sandra had done her homework; the trouble was I just didn't see her looking like Anne Boleyn. The curves under her mink looked suspiciously larger; I didn't remember her bust being so prominent. There was only one way forward and that was to be blunt.

"Pardon me for mentioning this Sandra, but have you had your boobs done?"

"How did you guess? To be honest, I've been a bit worried now I'm pregnant. There are too many horror stories, but my surgeon assures me everything will be fine."

The design Sandra favoured was the square-cut flattened bodice we had all seen in movies and television dramas. I wasn't surprised that she had found it difficult to get someone to make the thing up for her. The logistics of encasing silicon boobs was more an engineering feat than dressmaking.

"It's certainly a challenge," I said.

"But not impossible?" Sandra asked, a worried frown on her face.

"Not impossible," I replied. "A bit of ingenuity on my part should do the trick."

Flo asked another important question, "Have you got the fabric, or is that down to us?"

Here we go, I thought, and waited for a complex list of requirements. I had visions of tracking down a rare silkworm in the depths of China and asking it kindly to spin enough yarn to weave fifteen metres of fabric.

"I want ivory silk taffeta with gold brocade trim, and lots of petticoats."

"Very tasteful," Flo agreed.

Now I needed to talk about how much I was going to charge. I would get straight to the point. When we first started the business I used to worry about quotations, but these were different times. I wasn't going to sell myself short, not even for a friend.

"Three thousand including the fabric and all the trimmings, does that sound fair?"

Sandra's face did not flicker; I sensed she would have probably paid more.

"It's a deal," she said.

"This is so exciting I think it calls for a drink," Flo

said and went off to get the bottle opener.

"Don't even think about it," I called out to her. "I need to take measurements first and arrange a date for a fitting. And remember this bride-to-be is not allowed any alcohol."

Flo was about to argue but handed me my bag of tools instead. It took another half an hour of painstaking measuring, and I was surprised to find Sandra's bosom more impressive than I'd estimated. Her bra size was 42DD.

When we finished, I couldn't resist asking Sandra a few more questions. Flo had been correct about her being tight-lipped, and it was beginning to intrigue me.

"So who is the lucky man?"

"Sorry girls, but I'm afraid that information has to be kept quiet for the moment. All I can say is that you will find out after the wedding."

"Will we get an invitation as we are making the dress?" Flo enquired in a girlish tone.

"We're actually going abroad for the ceremony. It's going to be a very quiet affair with no fuss, only close family attending and that's all I can say. I made a promise." I continued my interrogation. "So who have you made a promise to?"

Sandra exposed her suntanned wrist and glanced at a sparkling watch. Something had made her jittery, and

I sensed she wasn't prepared to answer my question.

"I must be going, tons to do," she muttered and looked away from us.

Apart from tying her to the chair and shining a bright light in her eyes, there was no way to keep her. She gave us both a kiss on the cheek and ran out the door. Flo followed and I hoped she would keep quiet about our situation. I know my sister well and that can be worrying. This time I was sure she'd be too embarrassed. Flo doesn't cope well with uncertainty.

Over the next week, the weather improved. There was a rapid thaw followed by a hint of spring sunshine and, best of all, the prospect of some money. We were in marginally better spirits working on the dress and Sandra was excited about her first fitting. I deliberately left the bodice until last, as the technicalities of supporting Sandra's breasts were complicated.

Normally we would have used boning; not the old whalebones of yesteryear but the modern nylon stuff. However, in order to achieve the required look, I would have to build extra padding on the inside, much like building a wall. I was busy experimenting when Flo brought the tea and made a comment.

"I can't see those little bricks working."

I took the comment as a criticism and retaliated. "Back in 2000, a group of engineers used computer modelling software to design a bra. I'm attempting to be innovative, so give me some credit. If you can think of another way feel free to try, otherwise start machining the petticoats."

I covered the tiny pieces of foam with taffeta. Even though they wouldn't be visible, I had strict rules. All finishing off had to be very professional.

We completed the dress five days before the wedding. Sandra was elated, and I must admit she looked good. My earlier doubts about the Tudor-style dress vanished when I watched her preening in front of the mirror. She looked taller and slimmer. Underneath the bodice, a narrow corset helped to reduce her waist measurement by a couple of inches. Most of her impressive bosom was on show, and I think that delighted her more than anything else. I knew she'd feel uncomfortable, but it was only one day and, as they say, pride is painful. Another surprise: Sandra paid cash.

Inside Barclays I couldn't help smirking when I went to make the deposit. My euphoria was short-lived. The bank manager phoned later that day and said he wanted to see me.

Flo and I sensed an anticlimax after the dress. We turned up for work most days hoping the change in the weather would generate an increase in business. A month after we finished Sandra's dress, I noticed our haberdashery supplies were getting low, especially thread. I took a trip into town to replenish the stocks only to find there was a long queue in the shop. The girl in front of me was absorbed in a celebrity magazine. At first, I thought I was seeing things as I craned to look over her shoulder.

But I wasn't hallucinating at all; she was there in all her glory at the bottom of the front page.

Buying thread could wait. I sprinted across the road to the newsagents, praying they still had a copy. My luck was in. I clutched it tightly but resisted looking until I was back at the workshop.

'EX-RUGBY HERO JIMMY ANDERSON MARRIES SANDRA COOK AT FLORIDA HIDEAWAY.

'Jimmy Anderson, responsible for England winning the world cup eleven years ago, has married ex-girlfriend Sandra Cook. After a twenty-year separation, the couple bumped into each other six months ago at a mutual friend's 40th birthday bash. A whirlwind courtship followed, and when Sandra discovered she was expecting a baby, Jimmy proposed. The couple declared their delight at the prospect of becoming parents.'

Underneath the blurb was a group wedding photo. There were several more on the following page. Everyone was Hollywood glitz and over the top. I stared at Sandra's new hubby. I knew nothing about rugby, but his name was familiar and I remembered reading that after retiring from the game he had gone into show business and made a packet.

"Well, well," I said to Flo, "no wonder she couldn't say anything. I bet they got a fortune for this little lot. Notice there's no mention of who made the dress."

"No, just a description of the style and how beautiful she looked."

"With his dosh she doesn't need to worry anymore. Bloody hell, the reason she didn't tell us was because she knew we would have charged her a hell of a lot more." I couldn't help the resentful tone.

Flo looked hurt. "Don't say that Jude, she's a friend. I know it's a bit off, but she got what she wanted and she paid what you asked."

I closed the magazine. "If it wasn't for the dire financial situation I wouldn't have given a toss. Now she's married money she'll be off to the famous designers for her clothes. We served a purpose, Flo, and now we're history."

The visit to the bank manager turned into a lecture on the dangers of complacency. By the time he'd finished, my fragile optimism had disappeared, so I went round to Flo's that night to get drunk. When the bottles were empty, I asked Flo if I could watch the news before bed. It was the predictable depressing garbage, but as I went to switch off there was a breaking story, a report from Florida.

Rugby hero Jimmy Anderson had saved his wife in a swimming pool drama. The cameras were at the scene. The American correspondent stood outside a pink mansion on a leafy road. Apparently, the couple had thrown another reception for some of their friends who hadn't made it to the wedding. Sandra had worn her wedding dress for the event and later that evening, after the guests were gone, Sandra had fallen into the pool.

Jimmy heroically plunged in to save his wife. He wasn't a strong swimmer and had ended up in difficulties, but the bodice of the dress saved the day. The correspondent likened it to a "Mae West Vest", an early life jacket design which saved hundreds of pilots during the Second World War, including George Bush senior.

The report went on to say the light-weight foam fabric sewn into the top expanded, allowing Sandra to float until Jimmy got his act together. The couple were recovering in a nearby hospital. The cameraman panned to a "friend of the family", who explained how, when Jimmy was on his way to the emergency room, he insisted the real heroes were the designers of the dress. "They saved us," he had sobbed.

I added the silicon bosoms into the equation. By the law of averages they had to have helped.

"They didn't give our names," Flo said, disappointment in her voice.

"Think about it, she's a celebrity now. Why admit to having a couple of nobodies as your dressmakers. I bet she's too bloody embarrassed to say."

"You never know, it might be in the *News of the World* in the morning," Flo said hopefully. Sure enough, the following morning an article appeared on page three, but we were still anonymous. Nevertheless, I felt somewhat proud being a hero, even if it was only for one day. It had made a subtle difference to me and the future seemed less gloomy. Then another nice thing happened: Derek our landlord didn't want us to leave. I felt like crying when he said we could have a three-month rent-free period.

Flo went off to do something on the computer; she came back waving a piece of paper at me excitedly.

"I got an e-mail from Sandra. Here, read it."

"I can't find my glasses, I'll listen."

My sister launched into her posh voice with perfect enunciation. As kids, we had elocution lessons; suddenly I was back in another era, to Miss Ritchie's gloomy Victorian villa where Flo and I learned to recite long extracts from Shakespeare for exams.

"Jude, please pay attention."

"Sorry," I replied, "I was thinking of something else."

"Dear Flo and Jude," Flo repeated. "I hope you don't mind but I've sent my wedding dress back to you for repairs. I suppose by now you have heard what happened to Jimmy and me. I'm so stupid at times. Anyway, we won't be coming home until after the baby arrives. Could you make another dress in purple velvet with the same trim and send it back within the month? Oh, and make it a couple of inches bigger on the side seams. I need a new frock for a very special occasion we have coming up. Please find a cheque inside the parcel, it's from Jimmy, he's so very grateful, for very obvious reasons. We hope this amount will go towards helping you over your crisis. If not, let us know and we'll send some more. See you when I get back. Lots of love, Sandra."

"There you are. I knew she wouldn't forget about us," Flo said with a big smile on her face.

Where's Captain Kirk?
Aís

"You can't throw *me* to the lions, I'm Charlton *Heston*!"

Jim had always wanted to use that line by Jello Biafra. He instantly regretted it, more for the rising shout that got past his intended mutter.

Luckily, only a few hunched figures on the street nearby seemed to have heard him over the hiss of uncaring traffic as it ploughed on through the drizzle. The people just carried on too, preoccupied as usual with their own shit; Jim's outburst none of their business.

Damn right!

He turned a little unsteadily, then left the glistening tile exterior of The Mushroom Cloud in peace.

It wasn't really called that - except by him and his turncoat mates – because, just like in Langford's book the *Leaky Establishment*, The Wheatsheaf's sign looked quite like a mushroom cloud when you squinted at it.

Anyway, the lot of them were probably pissing themselves laughing in there, all at Jim's expense.

Got things to do anyway. He stumbled off, muttering in snatches to himself.

*

"Hey Jim, c'mon man. Open up in there, it's me, Lenny!"

One bleary eye forced itself open and registered the fact of daylight. Jim's head, though, felt too heavy to lift from the rough fabric of his broken-backed sofa.

His primal groan turned into: "Go away. Not up yet!"

"Wassat man, can't hear you?"

A pause from outside the door allowed other sounds some attention space for his subconscious to examine; general eleven-thirtyish-in-the-morning noises that came up from the street.

Jim rolled turgidly onto his back and let another, "Not up yet!" fly free and clear.

A briefer pause gave the bedsit time to stop spinning.

"I'll get us bacon butties then, eh? Back in ten, so get the kettle and some clothes on." The guffaw and asynchronous clatter of Lenny's departure down the stairs meant Jim now had some peace to face the day with.

He wasn't hung over, but lately he hadn't been able to get up like he used to. So it was closer to fifteen minutes before he managed to straighten up and stare at the kettle; willing it to life from where he lay. At that point he heard Lenny's returning footsteps, syncopated by his semi-asthmatic wheezing.

Jim got the door open before the anticipated

knock came. He hated inevitabilities that could be avoided.

"Hey, rough night?" Lenny held out a squishy packet full of promising smells which curled around him and crept ahead, into the bedsit.

Jim took it and sighed, expression wan and resigned.

Lenny checked the kettle's weight, added more water and clicked it on without a word. "So where did you get to last night, then? The lads said you just upped and left before I got to the meeting; all sudden like, no reason."

"Had stuff to do."

Lenny nodded and glanced over at the small kitchen table with its unchanged still-life of two mugs, opened pile of post and a saucepan with wooden spoon glued into the dried baked beans within. Tucked away behind the post, Jim's most recent bottle of pills from the doctor looked undisturbed since Lenny had last seen them five days ago.

He shifted his gaze slightly up to the window beyond, as if he could see something of worth through the slit where the landlord-provided curtains didn't quite meet. Lenny didn't want Jim getting into a state again, like he had last time he'd suggested he might have forgotten to take the damn things.

The silence settled; Jim wasn't the best conversation partner first thing in the day.

"Oh yeah. I remember...it was that *Trek* TV special you mentioned," Lenny prompted.

"No...Andreas Katsulas was in an episode of *Enterprise* – but that was jus' them tryin' to save a sinking ship I reckon."

"Sinking ship, like it! Plot-core meltdown!"

"Yeah – set scriptwriters on stun..." Jim was warming up in time with the kettle, and so Lenny grinned.

"That good, eh?"

"It was *Enterprise*! What more do you want me to say?"

Lenny struck a serious pose raising one eyebrow. "It's *Trek* Jim, but not as we know it!"

"Yeah, they're the Trekkers, and we're the Trekkies."

"Bloody Trekkers stole our limelight. But we know something they don't, eh? In Dutch, Trekker means wanker."

The kettle clicked off and Jim got up, smiling. "Thanks for that man, you're truly my Spock."

"Hah! Leonard and James: actor and character together against the universe!"

"Shame my real name's Rob then, isn't it?"

Lenny looked at him, but played along: "Yeah,

that's right! Saw it on your signing-on card once...so why *did* you change your name?"

"Dunno. One day I woke up and felt like I was more of a James than a Robert. It just sort of happened." Jim poured the water and reached for a spoon.

"Was that after you met the big-man himself at that Trek convention last year?"

Jim stopped in mid-teabag mash, and looked up, to the right. "Before, most definitely. Only by a few days though, maybe a week. Jus' seemed right."

"I wonder if ol' Bill Shatner will ever come back over here. The way things are going, it doesn't look like it. So, until that day comes, you'll hold the top spot in the group – the only one of us to have actually met and shaken the hand of Captain Kirk."

Jim twitched as if bitten, then shrugged before dousing the tea with milk. "I think he's scared to travel nowadays."

"What? Captain Kirk afraid of a trip across the Atlantic: a man on a five year mission across the galaxy? That's professional suicide for actors, what with films being done cheaper elsewhere now. So where did you hear that then?"

"Didn't hear it as such, I just got a feeling that they're *all* scared since September the eleventh. None of them seem to be travelling much now, something to do with reminding the Arabs that every other minority and race is in the original series, except theirs."

"Hah! Stick two sugars in mine there you weird, weird motherfucker."

*

"Why, why, why did I say that? And out-loud too!"

No answer was forthcoming from his subconscious, or any of the dim corners of his bedsit. There was definitely an air of anticipation about the room though. Jim screwed up his eyes, tight, willing pain upon himself as punishment for being so stupid.

Now they'll all get to hear about it and I'll be the laughing stock...once more.

Slumped in his chair at the window, he glanced at the tacky wall clock. Lenny had already been gone over an hour, but still he couldn't stop the scene from repeating itself inside his head.

Suddenly restless and in need of air, or at least something to do which would take his mind from the snickering building inside his head, he shot upright.

"Right! Outside now! Get moving! Go!"

The door, its chipped and frequently painted surface seemed to rotate to one side, then just as slowly back over to the other. It felt like he was on a boat, at sea.

His breathing quickened, vision beginning to do strange things. It wasn't just the door, but the whole room shifted like a slow-motion see-saw around his focal point, the gloomy bedsit fading back behind a heavy dimness.

Vertigo – no, not now!

Jim slumped backwards, hands gripping the table and chair as if afraid of slipping in either direction.

Aware as he did so that his hand on the table was touching the plastic tub of pills, he recoiled. *No, damn you!*

He felt fear. Once more the words in his head, the actions, were not his own.

"Oh shit..." He groaned and closed his eyes really tight as he fought for control.

The medicine withdrawal wasn't responsible, he knew it. Something else was in there, messing with his mind. It was *the* voice he fought, the *other* him, and he refused to give in to it. *I–will–beat–this!*

Above his ragged breathing, he thought he heard faint laughter, but it was gone before he could be sure.

Minutes stretched outwards into the pulsing darkness, until Jim felt his heart slow down again and return to almost normal.

No, it couldn't be the pills, he felt sure of that. He'd been on them for over a year; low dosage Elavil for his anxieties, so nothing special. The vertigo and other symptoms had begun in the last three months however, so Jim had stopped taking all medication.

Since then it had begun to worsen, not gradually, or even suddenly, but sporadically. This was how Jim knew that the pills hadn't been responsible.

He felt sure it was the voice that made him stop, though his memory was too hazy to be sure. It had certainly become stronger recently.

He didn't want to go back to the doctor though, to get something new instead. The sight of his case file always depressed him, a fat folder pregnant with twenty-eight years of bad news. He was sure the doc kept it around just to make a point, hefting the thing into view whenever Jim went to him for something. The surgery had been computerised for years, so why the folder, if not to make an unsubtle point?

"Feck the lot of 'em!" His sudden outburst reverberated within the room's confines, startling him. "I ain't goin' to buckle," he added in a softer tone.

The room seemed to have settled itself, so Jim got cautiously to his feet. He needed to get out for a while; the landlord had already spoken to him about random shouting and how that upset the other tenants, so he needed to be gone, just in case he came calling.

Another warning would be his last, and getting a new place at a price he could afford, that would be a pain he could do without just now.

Letting himself out quietly, Jim tip-toed down the stairs; with luck no one would hear him go. He could say he'd left with Lenny and so plausibly deny being at home if the outburst was reported. Taking a walk should limit the damage, as no fucker out on the street would care what he shouted, they never did.

*

Jeff hated the lunch-time shifts. *Either dull or dangerous was what they were; no middle ground at all, not in an old pub like this.* Trying to disguise that he was doing so, Jeff kept an eye on the lad nursing his pint over in the far window seat. Lunchtimes were when the walking-wounded felt safe enough to come out. Most would just sit in the shadows away from the regulars and daily drift-ins, then be gone before four; this one though, had begun muttering to himself.

"Is he alright?"

Jeff looked at the lunch-time regular stood on his usual spot at the bar. "Not sure. I'm keepin' an eye on 'im though, mate."

The punter turned to his workmate and chuckled. "Thought he'd had too much, that's all."

Old Sid, sat at the bar two stools away, shifted slightly before picking up his pint to work down another careful mouthful; just staring ahead in that disconcerting way he had. Jeff knew that very little escaped the old boy.

He had probably survived until now by doing just that, keeping quiet.

"Yeah, well don't go drawing attention to 'im. Like I say, I've got my eye on things."

Old Sid's nod of approval was subtle.

Ten minutes later, Jeff came around the bar to collect the few glasses left on the tables, still keeping the possible nut-job in sight as he went.

*

"Not good – not good..." Jim hunched in on himself protectively, hands clasped firmly around his now flat and unappetising pint.

He did this more to hide any signs of the shakes than fear of it being taken away from him by the approaching barman.

Don't be such a coward, man. Stand up and meet your adversary, square on!

"Not listening..." he muttered in answer to the voice now clear in his head. He was scared. It had never been so strong before. He even felt his body part-respond to the command.

Not listening...don't you try that Gollum *trick on me!*

"Not Gollum, I'm Jim..."

I can see it playing in your head, boy. I've seen it through your eyes – it–won't–work.

Jim let out a strangled moan, sweat standing clear on his brow.

"You okay there, mate?" The barman had stopped three feet before Jim's table, trying his best to look assertive, no-nonsense like.

"Y-yeah – fine, ta." Jim gripped his pint tighter and tried to look natural, even adding a small flick of his head to get a stray lock of lank hair out the way.

The man looked uncertain for a second. "It's only that someone said you were maybe talking to yourself..."

Jim looked down at the table-top and nodded. "On my mobile, hands-free, ain't I?"

The barman's expression was a mixture of relief along with embarrassment, glancing at the phone to cover himself.

He then looked back at Jim, eyes already hard. "So how come it's not turned on?"

"Hell..."

"I think it's time you left, eh? Don't want to be causing a scene and end up getting barred now, do you?"

"Yeah, okay." Jim got up slowly, reluctant as he was unsteady. "Reckon I could get a cab? I got money."

"Not a chance, mate. Maybe if you hadn't pulled that little trick just now. Jus' leave, an' we'll say no more about it, eh?"

"*Hab SoSlI' Quch!*" Jim spat the Klingon words out

just right, his minor victory carrying him past the surprised barman and out the door before there was any response.

Your mother has a smooth forehead? Where did you learn such language, boy?

"*Bljatlh 'e' yImev!*"

The voice chuckled in his head. *Oh, but I'm here to stay – and you're not Jim, I am – the one and only James Tiberius Kirk. All I want is to get out of your head and to go back home. Out there where I belong, boy!*

With a wail, Jim stumbled off down the street; head clutched in his hands, all but ignored by the early-afternoon crowd; just another casualty of the modern world.

This story appears with kind permission from Spizz and the band - should you be curious about their current happenings, you can find them at: www.spizz.eu or www.spizzenergi.com

# Side Two:

Simon Sees

Jacky Cowper

I'm a hero, I am. You should all be thanking me. But no one will ever know my name. It's safer that way.

As he wrote the words in his notebook, Simon looked them over, and thought long and hard about committing his thoughts to paper.

His scrawl was barely legible but, to him, the words stood out as clear as any typewritten script.

He fingered the silver metal ring on his middle finger. Its cold lightning bolt symbol stood out against his pale flesh. He ran his other hand over it and clasped it to his scrawny chest.

He knew that the fate of mankind rested on his too-thin shoulders, and he sighed. It was a burden he just had to carry. He had been chosen. He was a superhero.

From the moment his weak and frail frame was pushed out of his mother's ample body, some seventeen years ago now, he had been destined to look after the world. His every decision changed the life of someone, somewhere, on the earth.

He knew this, completely and utterly, and it had

been proven to him time and time again over the last few months. Ever since he had found the ring.

He thought back to that day with a mixture of pride, relief and horror.

He'd been about to go to school. He really had. But as he'd passed the sign to the park, two streets before the turn off for the school, he'd spotted the dog. It looked like Colin, a dog he'd had many years ago. Colin had run off, and Simon had spent many, many fruitless hours combing the neighbourhood streets, dog biscuits in his pockets and hope in his voice.

Three years ago his mother confessed that Colin had been run over by a car while Simon was at school. Simon had been devastated. He'd always secretly nurtured the hope that Colin might come back through the door again, and lie down in his usual spot at the foot of Simon's bed.

He knew that Colin would be a very old dog by now, but still he kept that hope alive. He'd seen the brown mutt that morning. "Colin?"

The cur hadn't responded, but continued sniffing at some unseen mark on the wall. It had allowed the boy to come closer, but trotted off to the next corner at the very last minute.

Simon had followed, desperate to get closer to the mangy creature. His mother had lied for years about Colin having run away. Might she also have lied about the dog having died?

Any thoughts of school disappeared. The dog continued to explore the long wall that led towards the entrance to the park, and Simon found himself in pursuit. It rounded the corner and trotted into the piece of scrubby greenery. Simon was only a few strides behind, but when he rounded the end of the wall the dog was nowhere in sight.

He stopped and examined the area carefully, poking his feet into the overgrown bushes. He even pulled himself up into a tree to scan the area. That's when he'd spotted the slightest flash in the crook of the branches. His grubby fingers pushed the moss aside – and brought out the ring.

He'd never seen any ring like it before. He had always considered himself a manly man. Rings were for girls. But this ring drew his eyes like no other. A plain silver band drew itself into a jagged lightning flash at either end, without meeting. Its double flash gave (he fancied) a 3D effect. This was clearly a man's ring. He slipped it on to the middle finger on his right hand, the only one it would fit.

He held his hand out at a distance, the better to admire the ring, and eased himself down onto the ground. The dog was gone. He knew that Colin had come back from doggy heaven to lead him to the ring.

He was too late for school now – he'd heard the flat tone of the bell as he'd been rooting around looking for the dog – so he decided to have a day to himself. He would examine his new treasure.

If he gave it half an hour, he could slip in back home. His mum would have left for her shift at the supermarket and he'd have a few hours with the telly before she got back in. He might even make her some beans on toast, as a treat. That'd sweeten the old bat.

On the way home, Simon realised he had developed the power to curse people.

An old man had pushed past him in his haste to reach the bus stop. Simon stumbled and spat at the crooked figure.

"Blind old fool," he yelled. Seconds later, the elderly man had tripped on a paving stone and tumbled full length onto the pavement. Simon stood, his mouth agape, as a couple of passing mothers stopped to help the old chap back to his feet, dusting him off and picking up his white stick – a stick Simon would have sworn wasn't there seconds before...

Over the past year or so he'd begun feeling he had a special power. Sometimes he could see things that other people couldn't.

Six months before, he'd spotted two pirates

engaged in a deadly duel, cutlasses crashing together with considerable force – and noise – in the school playground. Simon had been in English class at the time. It was Shakespeare, and he was bored. He'd happened to glance out of the window – and seen the pair, going at it as if they were auditioning for the next *Pirates of the Caribbean* film.

The fight ended when the tall thin one missed a thrust, and the shorter but heavier man with the patch parried the sword and stuck a thin knife right into the other man's guts. Simon was surprised that there wasn't more blood, but when he looked round quickly to see if anyone else had spotted them, they disappeared. He hadn't been frightened, more puzzled. During the next school interval, he estimated where the pair had had their struggle to the death and examined the spot on the gravel where he thought they'd been, but there were no signs of anything out of the ordinary. Some of the other boys called out to him.

"Simple Simon!"

"Simon Strange!"

One or two gave him a quick kick in the legs, just for fun.

The jeers were familiar, and easy to ignore. He'd grown up with them.

The pirates had probably fallen through some interdimensional wormhole, and disappeared back into their own reality when he'd turned away for a moment. Simon liked science fiction. It answered many questions, and he was pretty clued up about wormholes.

It seemed clear to him that the power of his mind had held them there, brought them through the porthole and kept them visible until he'd looked away, breaking the connection.

About a fortnight after the 'pirates incident', he'd been browsing the internet during an IT lesson and had spotted a photograph of a crashed passenger jet. With a start, he realised that that was exactly what he'd dreamed about the night before.

He could remember it all now: the scream of the engines, the wail of the fire engines as they raced across the tarmac, the smell of burning aviation fuel. Plainly his wild, dream-state ramblings had caused the plane to crash – killing all thirty-three passengers.

Since then he'd become increasingly aware that he was different from the other youngsters around him. He was gifted and special in a way no one could suspect.

*

He tried to limit the amount of time he spent asleep. He didn't want to cause any more plane crashes. There was a train collision in China, but he couldn't remember dreaming about that and, anyway, no one was killed, so perhaps he'd managed to change the dream to have a less violent conclusion. Forewarned is forearmed, he reckoned.

The ring, he knew instinctively, had something to do with his gift. Why else would Colin have led him to it?

He vowed to be careful what he said in future – the old guy had been lucky. Say Simon had shouted something really final, like "Drop dead!" He would have been a goner.

Simon swayed a little. His power was dizzying. But he knew he had to control it, otherwise, like so many of his comic book heroes, it would end up controlling him. He would use it for good – to protect people.

And he'd tried to, over the days, the weeks that followed. It was hard, but he liked to think he made a difference.

A few weeks ago, as he walked home from the shops, he'd seen a drain cover move. There was a dark mark at one side which needed investigation. As he got closer, he realised that what he had taken to be a stain was in fact a hand. A nasty gnarled hand, clawing its way up from the bowels of the city.

Quickly, he did the only thing he could think of, and jumped with all his weight on top of the cover. There was a ghastly muted scream from inside the hole as the creature desperately pulled its hand in again. Grimacing, he stamped even harder on the metal lid.

"Don't you ever, EVER think about coming up topside again!" he yelled at the drain cover. He didn't care that he was shouting out loud – the monster had to be taught a lesson.

People stared and gaped. He could hear their muttered words of disapproval, but that was nothing new. Simon was way past caring about a few looks or sideways glances. He stared intently at the ground by the cover, and was satisfied that the dark mark was just scratches left behind as the creature scrabbled to withdraw its hand. A small, dark patch of troll blood remained on the metal edge.

Another job well done. He stepped off the cover and carried on along the street. On the windowsill of a flat above a newsagent, he spotted a canary in a cage. It was a beautiful shade of yellow. The bird looked at him, its beady black eyes fixed on his pale face.

"You can see them now," it sang.

He must be hearing things. But as he looked at the bird, it spoke again.

"You're so strong now, the ring has given you the power to see."

"What do you mean?" he asked.

"I can't say too much," the bird trilled, its head darting from side to side. "But you can see them now. The ring has given you that power. It's in their eyes. Watch their eyes."

Its message came to a halt as a hand emerged from the open window and lifted the small cage back in.

A middle-aged woman glanced out at the strange young man having a conversation with her bird, and watched as he walked on again, past her house.

She shook her head slightly and then closed the window again. Just Simon, she thought. He was an odd lad. Always had been. The whole family was weird.

Simon was aware she had been looking at him. The ring brought all his senses, all his latent powers, to the surface. He could feel the pavement beneath his feet. He could hear every car engine as it sagged along the road. He could even hear the voices of all the people who were brushing past him in the street. Anger, dissatisfaction, envy. Their thoughts were all ridiculously the same. No one was happy any more. The faces told a million stories of lives half-lived and lessons never learned.

He smiled at them as they went by. They should be happy. He was here now, protecting them. They were lucky and they didn't know it.

When he'd reached his home, he'd spent the afternoon examining the ring further – without taking it off, of course. It glinted in the gathering darkness of his house and the flash seemed to be alive with energy. He poured some beans into a pan and heated them on the stove until they were warmed through.

He heard the gate squeak at the foot of the path, and shoved two slices of white into the toaster.

His mother trudged wearily into the living room. Simon stood ready, with one plate of hot food in hand.

"Oh thank you, Simon," she said. "What a lovely treat. Shove on the telly, son."

She pulled off her coat and laid it over the back of the sofa. Dropping into the sagging cushions, she kicked off her shoes.

Feeling comfy, she turned round to Simon and reached out for the plate, another smile lighting up her doughy face. "You're a good lad when you want to be."

Simon smiled at her, pleased to have been praised. His smile froze as he looked at her.

It's in their eyes...

The words came flooding back as he looked into his mother's face. In the dancing light thrown by the TV, he saw what the bird had meant.

His mother's pupils, instead of being round, were slits in the colour, like those of a sheep. He'd seen weird eyes before – David Bowie, Ziggy Stardust himself, had one big pupil and one normal one; the result, so they said, of an accident when he was a child – but not like these.

Of course, the logic was instant.

They'd known all about him, known how special he was, right from the start. They'd replaced his mother with one of their own, all the better to watch him.

Play it cool. Don't let them know you're on to them.

"No problem," he said, handing her the plate and watching carefully as she thrust the soggy meal into her mouth.

Now he was playing a waiting game. He watched his mother – no, the creature that was passing itself off as his mother – go about her normal business. He kept a note of everything in his notebook. He kept the notebook hidden under the mattress. She wouldn't look under there. He began to draw up his plans. Since he was the only one who could see them, then it would have to be him that dealt with the creatures.

He went to school as usual and kept an eye on the newspapers. All the time he was learning how to use his powers, and just how strong they were. He learned to live with the numbing pain when he read of another car crash or fire, where people were hurt. He learned that if he snapped a book shut in a temper, a tornado would hit a small town in Kansas. If he shouted at someone, then very soon after some mishap would befall them. He could not discern a pattern to the 'crime' or the 'punishment' – some of the most serious 'offences' seemed to draw the least significant pay-back – but he took consolation in the fact that there were at least some consequences.

His mother had mentioned his new ring, but had accepted his explanation that it was a tribute to a new pop group he was keen on.

She doesn't seem to suspect, he thought.

Life became a quiet desperation for him, as, no matter how well he tried to behave, disasters kept happening. It seemed that somewhere in the world, someone always died because of something he did.

He found it almost impossible to sleep. He didn't dare dream. He couldn't control his dreams. He was ratty much of the time, which caused him to lose his temper and act up. Every time he did, he would groan inwardly. There goes another family somewhere, he'd remind himself as another mood swing took him. The newspapers would confirm his theory. A fire here. A drowning there. And when he was excluded from school for refusing to leave the cloakroom after he stood on a spider, a whole ferry went down off Thailand…

It was on his head. He had to get away, leave the crowded city and the life he had known behind. Step out into the world where no one knew him.

The ring was a curse, and a gift. With power came responsibility indeed.

He knew he had to leave. He spent the afternoon packing a small rucksack with essentials. His mother had been angry when the school informed her that he'd been excluded for absenteeism, but he had kept his cool, been unmoved by her temper. He had to. The fate of the world depended on him.

Her slit eyes flashed at him and he had to bite his tongue to stop himself from blurting out that he knew what kind of monster she really was. Inwardly he wept for the loss of his real mother. He had never felt particularly loved, but at least she had been his. He could not tell them he could see them.

Who knew what they would do if they knew his abilities had been awakened?

Half an hour before she was due home, he began the process of preparing her evening meal. This time he opened a can of mini sausages and beans as well as doing the toast. She'd like that.

When he heard the familiar squeak outside, he pushed the handle of the toaster down and waited for it to pop.

She clumped in to the living room, dumped her heavy coat over the settee and eased her shoes off. Her familiar routine.

Simon was ready with her tray and offered it to her. He watched, pleased, as she took it gratefully and began to eat.

"Simon," she said. "This is lovely, a real treat. But

you've forgotten the sauce."

"Sorry Mum," he said, and disappeared into the kitchen.

He found the sauce bottle in the pantry and the boning knife in the drawer. He walked through to the small room, lit only by the light from the screen in the corner.

"Who's that on the telly?" he asked, handing the bottle from behind her.

She looked up, squinting to try to make out the presenter of the quiz show.

"Oh, that's–"

She got no further. The razor-sharp blade sliced through arteries and voice box in a single, strong cut.

Simon pushed her neck down towards her chest and watched in fascination as the blood spattered, heaved and gurgled down her body and across the room. The tray crashed to the floor as she jerked, tomato sauce hitting the TV screen and mixing with the blood on the glass.

He gripped her head and held on, waiting for the limbs to lose their power. The body twitched spasmodically.

Within two minutes, she was dead. The sitting room an abattoir.

At least I can kill them, he thought. He washed his

hands in the kitchen sink. He'd done his research properly. The beauty about a forward projection of arterial blood was that anyone behind the body would not be sprayed.

"All you had to do was bring back my mum," he said to the corpse, pale and unmoving, still staring at the ever-chattering TV.

He slept fitfully that night but, luckily, didn't dream.

Next morning he pulled on his jacket and left the house, carefully closing the door behind him. His school uniform lay abandoned in his wardrobe. He was finished with that life now. He checked in on his mother, but she was still exactly as he'd left her the night before. Good, he thought. No zombie resurrection, then – though the room smelled bad enough.

He wasn't sure if killing one of them would count as a good or bad deed, but if it went against him, then a major conflict would surely break out somewhere.

He allowed his feet to choose his path, and after twenty minutes found himself back at the park where it had all begun. It seemed like a lifetime ago now.

He looked at the tree and eased himself back up into the branches again, the better to take in the view and decide where to go next.

It was a beautiful day. The sun was shining, the park making the most of the modest light it was offered.

As he looked round, wondering what to do, a small bird landed a short way from his head and caught his attention.

"It's too much for one person to bear," it said, holding Simon's gaze with its small, black eyes.

"I tried, I really did. I wanted so much to be a hero, but I couldn't stay good." A tear pushed its way out from under his long lashes. "I got one of them – just one."

"I know," said the bird, pulling a berry from the twig it perched upon. "One is better than none. But now that you've killed one, the rest will come to you. You don't have to look any more. Just sit still and play their game, then kill them when you get the chance. You'll see I'm right."

With that, it twitched its wings and flew into the sky, leaving him alone with his thoughts. Simon's head began to nod. It was peaceful in the tree. Warm and pleasant. He dozed off.

He was still there that evening, sitting in the tree, watching the sky, when the police found him. They had a pair of male nurses with them. The men helped him from the tree and eased him into an ambulance. One left to drive while the other stayed with him.

He noticed, with interest, that the man had slits instead of pupils.

Simon smiled.

Hotel C.N.S

Marc Nash

Ow! Unyielding. World already in total darkness, now shrunk to two foot at the end of a chain. Ha, the length of a cubit, more like. Tight against...like...a radiator. It's so damn hot here, who'd ever need a radiator for godssakes? Ow! Cuffs cutting into me. My flesh interposed between metal on metal. The weak link. Have to stay perched at the correct angle. An involuntary movement and immediate barbaric retribution! No, I came here to teach these people to repair themselves. And this is how they treat me? Tethered like an animal. At least the painted metal's cooling, I suppose. Let's see if I've any movement at all here. Yes, if I just slide along this pipe, got my very own exercise yard. Have to keep remembering to give myself permission to move. Private Hell reporting for duty in someone else's war, Sir!

Clearly I have been afforded a window. The region of sight. Mocking me. Least it means I'm no longer in a cellar. Still in the pockmarked ruins of the city even? If I can just...Sun's definition, without luminescence, so only heat and fatigue to guide me. Got it. Full on now. Bob my face minutely across the arc of its gaze...How clean the air feels...Up in the mountains, or down in the desert? Who can tell? Cannot see, yet I am not blind. Have to keep telling myself that. Blindfold merely gnomon on the sundial of my skin. Time marked by coruscation, serves as my flare of distress. And listen out for sounds to narrate my story for me. All one need's contained in the distant artillery. Meeting as intended, or just recoiling? Then nothing but evaporated silence. Are my gaolers even in with me? Tied to my anchor in here, beneath the unfailing scrutiny of such a powerful daytime flashlight out there, they have no need of perpetual watchfulness.

Jesus, this damned heat! It's like a wall of steam. Can't even divine the sun directly on me anymore. Jiggle my head this way and that...Just so till it breaks the surface tension and the droplet leaps to freedom...or oblivion. And still the water trapped in the radiator watches on in impassive silence. *Deus otiose*. While my body performs its whirling dervish dance within the confines of a few inches. 'Scuse me, some mistake here, my bandana's slipped down over my eyes! It's not performing its function. Nowhere for the refugee beads of perspiration to go. I don't actually believe I have any captors. Can't see them, can't hear them and, despite living in close proximity inside a Turkish bath, I can't even smell them. They simply don't exist. But I know how to make them jump! Just remove my blindfold. Or look as though I might. Mop my brow and get pistol-whipped to death for my pains. Technological update of a stoning. I was wrong about these people and their primitive methods. They've had coaching, from our side. End it all, here and now. It would be quicker than drowning. And all for a bead of sweat, truly about a pound of my dissolved flesh.

*

Christ, it's freezing! I never knew exactly how cold it could be. In the desert, or up in the mountains. Now I know why there's a radiator. Thank god for small mercies. For my constant companion, when before I cursed you. Warmed where my body presses against it, while the other side remains chilled to the marrow. Have to keep turning myself, like toasting a piece of bread, only I will never be done. Cuffs no longer rend flesh with sawing mass, but merely by an icy kiss. My country, why has thou forsaken me? Seems the value of my life has lapsed way beyond any useful deadline. Since my heavenly clock has also been arrested, I am utterly beyond counting time. Beyond anything, other than just concentrating on complete stillness beneath my blankets. To prevent cold air's brutal rupture. Yet through such numbness, one part of me still protests palpable sensation. Hands wringing unwittingly, as if seeking to draw the pain from my wrists. Tenderly pricks as to freshly tilled corporeality; peel back through the fantastic fibrinogenous weave garnering logistics; back, back, to bathe in the cascading fountain of clotting factors; and see DNA's sequential metamorphosis, as each lock finds its key and my skin repairs the breach of its metal siege engines. Fancy meeting God at the Hotel du C.N.S. And out of season, too.

**

All activity in the world ceases. Except for one, that of watching. And of being watched. I thought, at least with this feeble heat to share, there might be some contact with my silent gaoler. Back home, when I wasn't fleeing it, you were never quite alone. What with the old pipes chuntering or gurgling and the groaning Victorian timber. All the life within those walls, staying up to keep you company, playing tricks on you...always thinking there's some spook moving about in the room, or some thief in the night. But here, an even older building I surmise, yet not a single sound. And how does heating on full blast stay so quiet? A superior design in everything? Or perhaps manifests another difference between us. Where our god is an absentee landlord, leaving priests and prophets to collect the rent, theirs demands the true reverence of forever being in his presence. To move with catlike grace, wasting no energy that otherwise could be used for devotion. They tread so silently, that I am unaware of them being in the room. Until they are upon me with food or other tasks. Surely, if they have taken me hostage, they should at least instruct me as to their reasons? Perhaps even try and win me over to their cause? Now, they may well not speak English, while I know I have no proficiency in their mother tongue, but between us we must be able to swap a few words of French? Yet nothing. They have uttered not a single word since I came here. Quite unlike that other bunch of gangsters in the city. They needed me to justify their cause, to ordain them as captors and vindicate their violence. But this bunch...There is something about them, though. Had thought they might be nomads, tending flocks in the desert. But they stay so immutable here, that cannot be correct. Then they could be hill farmers, but surely goats would elicit more mindfulness than shown me. It's like I don't even exist for them in their lives at all. And I'm forced to start agreeing. An absent presence.

    They give me my bed pans or piss pots and gently rub me down with wet cloths, taking care to avoid chaffing my bed sores. Kind without being compassionate, I would say. Yet despite knowing me so intimately, they give no trace of a flicker of response. They are not automatons, since their touch is more like that of women's hands, though I know them to be men, for there are never any seasonal smells brewing. Who, who are they and why will they not reveal themselves? They are like the eunuch mutes of old, unable to ask any questions, able to tell no lies. So heaven knows what their superiors, the fundamentals at the top, are like. All I know is that my country will not be able to entreat with them. Even if it were of a mind to. For I sport this blindfold on its behalf. It does not see me as one of its citizens, but as a principle. It will not deal with terrorists and freedom fighters. Unlike the bloody French, of course! These men do seem to be from a much older culture. One that has survived countless assaults. And suddenly I feel irredeemably hopeless. Though serviced well, I will never have any semblance of relationship with them. And that in itself is crushing. But also to know that my nation will never defeat them. Will never move these disciplined troops from beyond their task. That is annihilating.

***

Forever this wretched heat! Invisible torturers keep feeding more water on the coals. Browbeaten by my own sweat. So who needs bleeding gaolers when you're trapped inside a bubble of steam? Sitting on my stomach, pressing down on me, no matter which way I move. My back awash in the pool of my shirt and both submerged within a wider ocean of the mattress. Primed senses now have absolutely no sense of themselves or my body. No longer even the coolness of the radiator to the touch, for I too am full of dull vapours. Yet there is one petrified imprint by which to record the fissure of time. Perspiration no longer gathers in the guttering across my brow. Rather now abrades a channel down into the orbits of my eyes. Scorched earth as I withdraw into the narrow depression beyond. Eroding ever deeper, it will not be denied its source. Till it has beaten a path to my tear ducts and demands them to break the banks of their accommodating reservoir. Simply cannot weaken to it. I am a pillar of salt and must dissolve were I to look back and long for what I once had. Even my skin seems to have extinguished its healing torch, choked and congealed behind a permanent dam of scar tissue. Oh god, here it comes! I'm-going-to-die-never-get-out-of-here-leave-this-place-never-experience-pleasure-again-all-previous-counts-for-nought-wiped-clean-as-in-death-itself-never-wake-up-and-never-know-haven't-woken-like-this-imprisoned-life-non-life-itself-arrrgghhh! Welcome hysterical torrent. Leapfrogging over itself. Blot out all thoughts overload, nail down and shroud with a deep drift of snow, hold myself together. Oww! To cover my ears hurts my wrist, pain brings relief to focus on. To return me to this. Peaceful co-existence with myself. Feel like a man in hospital, his eyes swaddled in bandages after being operated on, who doesn't know if he will recover his sight. Only, my whole being has been excised, amputated. Though my mind still feels its ghostly manipulations.

I have been transfixed, leading life bolted on to my nerve ends, craning for any sensory impression at all. Like a Medieval mind, trawling through the void, expecting to vanish off the earth at the horizon. Ears straining in the silence to make out any rustle, now conjure up their own inner noise. Tinnitus chaperones me. My eyes peer into the constant suspension of the blindfold, anticipating it at any moment to become a cinema screen for my own private projection. My body the frontier of meaning across which nothing is exchanged. So only feeling can possibly remain. I could just reach out and touch him. When he isn't expecting it. When he comes to shave me perhaps. Hand poised to lather me, I could just brush his arm, it would be so easy. He'd be forced to acknowledge me. His muscles might stiffen at another human being's contact. But then what would his response be? Would he club me? Would I be condemned to grow a beard? Pondered on this for weeks, keeps my mind in a state of relative calm. Weighing up the pros and cons. Rational decision-making, almost. It would break up the monotony, something would necessarily have to change. Christ, why not just do it, for goodness sake! Goddamnit! No! He couldn't. Somehow, after all those months of the same...he'd read my intention to change. And he'd read it before the intention had even communicated itself to my body. I could try again, next time, or a month hence, but always he'd be alert. I'd never get to touch him. So much for feelings. They still require both to be housed, and to have an object to lavish on. Body to body. Where neither resides in this place.

****

There is one outpost that yet reports. Oh, delicious irony! My finger where a wedding ring used to be. It registers a violated boundary, a swelling. No, not plundered by those city bandits. Just, in my own petty selfishness, I have hardly given a thought to you, my love. Thus as it ever was. Mad dogs and Englishmen...Why did I leave you to come here? Ach, you see how deceitful memory is? Because we'd already left each other for good, that I came here. You'd had enough of my wanderings and who can blame you? Every city where I went to ply my trade, I went without thought for you. Bravely you followed, strange countries with stranger tongues, often looking down on you for your sex. And when you'd commanded respect, I snatched it away, pulled up our tents and set off again for an unadulterated dominion of the male mind. Men of god who journeyed to those god-forsaken places, merely went by the book. Re-enacting Daniel in his lions' den, or Jonah and his whale. Having no such comfort of faith, I went of my own free will. Why? Why did I always have to move? Kidded myself that I was only to navigate by stars in a sky unvarnished by streetlamp sodium. To pursue their endlessly shining, undeluded truth. Well, now I have been dashed on the rocks of Scylla and Charybdis and washed up in a warzone. Only this time, no one waits on me. I have no right to request, to trade on our shared history, but will you remain my faithful Penelope, spinning a thread of hope? Burning a candle and keeping my memory alive in the world? But what right have I to ask you to banish suitors and put your life in mothballs? Even if we were still man and wife, it would be consigning you to a living death. Never knowing for sure whether to mourn without a body. I am glad you were able to re-enter life before my, er, peremptory deletion from it. So, why only now an overwhelming longing? I am beyond desire. All I have is habituated memory, snapshots. For memory becomes stasis.

I can't accommodate such a flow of thoughts all the time. Need a break from my mind grinding itself and me into the dust that doesn't even exist in the room, though I have shed countless skins. But there is no respite, not even at night, since then it drives febrile dreams. I imagined that it would cease its intensity, as rage and prospects faded, while the past no longer intruded. Indeed, I would welcome such stupor. But no, my mind sets out its stall to watch over me all the time. As if I needed another overseer. No longer filled with the bulk of my body, it manufactures a tide of thoughts to keep itself company. How about what I want for a change? A little peace. Peace. Peace...Of course! I've got it. They're not soldiers, but monks! An ascetic discipline, from a far more ancient age. Jungle-engraved temples now long reclaimed, or those cultures etched on stoneface in detail as profuse as the slave populations who worked them. What am I saying, they are those bas rolicfs! Caryallds, no Telamons, but ushering witness to what arcane wisdom beyond?

*****

I don't believe it! I can see through my blindfold. Nothing too detailed, just shades of light blunted through salt island refractions. Sweat must have bleached the material, worn it away. They wash every part of me and all my clothing, but the blindfold is never touched. A small triumph for the forces of light, then. Ha! At last, a flaw in construction. The portents were all aligned. For the paint on the radiator has blistered too. I can make out the warp and weft of the cloth, see how it's fabricated. Each stress, follow the way of the world for me to recreate it. Plot the cartography. Time to regain a sense of myself, to reclaim the skin from fusion with the cuffs, to feel the shirt against my back. And finally to confront the face of my gaoler and turn his...Arghh! Too much light, blinding! He sees through me. Steel visor not silk veil. So sharp, he illuminates the blood vessels to my eyes. That is too powerful. Too much focus. Too red. Brain's emptied of all but colour. Queasy. I fai-

Inky blackness. Shift change again. Black still as absence. Of colour. Of consciousness, of life. Of my gaoler who has gone elsewhere. I tried to shackle the sun to do my bidding! But he brought my blood to the surface to remind me of my frailty. Am I to settle for the company of my blackguard? He whom I never see? No one blackens me, for I do that to myself. But everything reddens me, stabs at me with little pinpricks of guilt. And since it is the underside of my flesh which so burns, I must be doing it to myself. Therefore I have some measure of control. Yet it was perspiration that partially restored my sight. It could have been tears, should have been, perhaps. And, with this underwhelming flood of sensations, comes also a new inner sense, of touch. Of pressure in this on-sided vacuum. That of tumescence.

For some time now I thought I was feeling it. Growing. Not at the one enduring site of skin regeneration, where you might expect the locus of cell over-stimulation. But rather populating the ruins of my mind. Push, push pushing all the time. Pathology of energy. Mutinous mutation. Let's face it, it's hardly the external environment that's carcinogenic now, is it? Maybe the tumour's merely at the place where a gun-barrel first touched my head and encouraged my mind to run amok on the other side. But no, I moved beyond fear eons ago. Strange how, having withdrawn from the world, I am undone by a lack of inhibition. All those foot soldiers conscripted by the mind in order to see off the body, now champing at nothing. As your doctor, I'd recommend...Oh god! I'm drowning! Sweat's running riot all over my face. I'm drinking it in. My brow's proud Maginot line no longer holds the invaders at bay. Why give me my sight back now, when the blindfold was protecting me? Brown leathered skin stretched tight across the sockets. Deep shafts mined out. Highlights the architectonics. A mirror onto the true shape of the skull beneath my face and that's more than any man should be allowed to see of himself. It's only right that I am ravaged from within. Nothing exists, not even me and I have had to conjure myself up. To keep me occupied from maudlin thoughts. But, of course, I could not possibly control it. Possessing me, filling me up with myself. Obsessed. Always thinking about number one. World peace anyone?

******

So what covenant of theirs is it that awaits my signature? Stare hard, scrutinise the space where their faces should be, for some sort of clue...And nothing. That must be the key, then. To enter their absence. That which has so threatened my mind up till now, must be the source of my redemption. No blindfold need weaken for me. I perceived it to be lighter, because I heard the sunrise. No, that's ridiculous. Am I finally going mad? But what if I've been granted my own cloistered cell as this special gift. No, not cell, too loaded a word. Hermitage, to anchor an anchorite. No noise and no movement, where time has been stopped for me. An opportunity to become timeless. To move at the pace of the mountains. No, that implies grandeur. To move at the pace of a grain of sand in the desert, before it is swept up by the wind in a storm and lost for ever. Why not, when each layer of sensation, experience and memory, has been progressively stripped from me and revealed the degrees of my unhappiness?

Finally worked out where I am. Where I've always been, in that desert wilderness. Maybe those weren't rockets I heard scudding to the ground, but pollen grains. To wait patiently forty years for the life-affirming waters to yield them birth. This is no ordeal, but a homecoming, for my exiled being. I must take as my guides the men who have been placed here to watch over me. These peaceable witnesses. They draw from deeper wells, of silence. Rise above my petty selfish concerns, and those gods and states we set over and between ourselves. Easier said than done, of course. For one didn't have to assume the lotus position, manacled to a bloody great radiator, back at the adult education institute. The sound of one hand clapping, anybody? Now, how did it go?

Think, or rather don't. Banish all thoughts and just breathe...

I'm hungry. That's not a very good start. S'posed to get beyond all that...

I'm hungry! I can't help it. I really am. Craving, a desire. Progress of a sort? Regaining my body, even if complainingly. I can feel all my joints aching, makes it hard to focus. Come on now, these thoughts get you nowhere. Must get beyond thoughts. And desire. Deeper. Hush, then! Withdraw and yield the periphery to the enemy that forever calls my name to attention and tugs me from my path. Hold out for silence, not sound.

At last I have it. Stillness. I note the white noise in my head, as it chats with my body, but all that is now background. The cocktail bar at the Hotel du C.N.S. Sharper yet are sounds around me. No, not sounds. Vibrations. Flitterings, trails in the air. Rhythmic, several, at different rates. Feel the silence, not just its rhythm, but its pitch and timbre too...Shapes a presence. Like a threshold to...Breath? I've unfurled their breathing? Pulsing together, like we are breathing for this whole room. For the land outside the window. Like we are breathing...underpinning the whole world. And we all breathe in freer air, up in the clouds. Was that a smile I smelt upon their faces?

I have my host more clearly before me now. His

shimmering outline, at least, for he appears to have no solidity. A field of dancing light. Wielding a scimitar, trailing a beauteous spectral wake as he parts the air. Not a scimitar, now that I taste its colour, a floppy green. It's a flower stalk! A long-stemmed bloom, held taut like steel. He has raised his vibration to that of a plant, so you cannot tell where one ends and the other begins. All is a swirl of energy. Realising itself and each other and then they are gone, floating beyond a place in time. Instructs as to my shattered soul, how my body declared war on me. Formerly so used to preaching resistance through pills, and imagining chemical magic missiles being hurled against the tumour. But to do so would only pitch my mind further against me. So I have to range deeper than visualisation. Metastasis. The cancer constantly recreating itself afresh, constant grooved motion utilising the cell machinery. Infiltrates the pulses. Time to re-appropriate the code. The work of intelligence agents behind the lines, rather than armies going to war. But intelligence contains memory, and memory runs the murderous programme. Only consciousness precedes intelligence, so strive to reach and change it. Working silently, beyond where disease can sustain, in the peace zone. Solely there can one meet consciousness. It is not for my selfish end that I devote myself to harmony. For the heart is to remain a citizen there, not just a tourist with a visa.

****

Scent of the baker's kneading hands. More often than not, that of a woman's. She has washed in the river and collected lavender to perfume her house, but the faintest traces cling to her hands as she makes the bread. And I marvel in her husband's dexterous threshing of the wheat, the grains so fine. A skill that goes back almost to the origins of creation. And I take it back further, to the heads of wheat growing so sparse under this fierce sun that bakes us all. How at night, it sways in the gentle breeze of the mouthed prayers of the farmer and his wife, hoping that the next day it will not be culled by the locust, but merely settled upon by a beautiful butterfly. Some days I trail it back yet further, back to the seedling that contains the whole of mankind within its kernel. How it unfolds its myriad connections to each and every one of us, even while still below ground. We put our trust in its mystery and are rewarded with a sense of our own continuous being modelled within. Now do you feel God's hand pull on you? You do? Then we shake our walls of isolation to the ground. Can you make out the silent horns of Jericho? See the pitiful proportions of the rubble of our lives as we step over it. We have become truly infinite.

What, so soon? But I need more time here.

The Canadian
Karen Snape-Williams

The funeral is over. I walk from the kitchen and into the hall, my footsteps echoing on the slate floor, resonating across rooms soothingly empty. All evidence of my guests has been removed. Only the curtains in the sitting room remain undisturbed. Respectfully closed, blocking out the afternoon sunlight normally engulfing this room.

I consider the period I should be seen to mourn Hugh, and surmise those who knew of our relationship will not expect me to suffer the indignity of feigning grief. I walk to the window, grasp the cord and the curtains open. It is done with.

*

A week has passed since the funeral. I collect my coat from the boot room. It is an old, tattered duffel left behind by Jack. Far too big, of course, yet it comforts me to wear it. In the study, I unlock the desk drawer and remove the box of letters. A soft knock and the door opens. Dilys, my housekeeper glances across to the box. Her eyebrows lift. Her mouth tightens. She touches the sleeve of my coat and frowns.

"Your coat is still damp from your walk yesterday.

Shall I fetch another, the black tweed perhaps?"

"No. This is fine."

"It won't take a moment."

"For goodness sake stop fussing, Dilys."

As I cross the veranda and descend the steps into the garden, I am already regretting my behaviour. I can at least acknowledge my irreverence following Hugh's death upsets Dilys. His illness has made its mark upon her and she is struggling to readjust. The beam of her searchlight is turning back to me, illuminating the widow who refuses to mourn.

September has slipped into October, the colour of summer long since gone. The garden is almost asleep, an easterly wind channelling fallen leaves along paths and onto borders where only the hardiest cling to life. There is a place in the garden where I have always found solitude. A gravel path surrounding a patchwork of allotments leads to a steep bank, at various times of year studded with snowdrops and anemones. Each step takes me further into a wilderness, a place where naked branches now droop under an abundance of hips and berries.

A garden seat, if it can be given so grand a title, for it is no more than a collection of wooden planks held together by rust and layers of flaking paint, is found behind this tangle of shrubbery. It is here I sit and place the box on my lap, remove the lid and select an envelope from the bottom of the pile.

Jack's initial letters are written with care. The words neatly spaced. It would not remain so. As the war progressed and the periods between sorties were reduced to moments, fear and exhaustion manifested itself in his thoughts, hopes and eventual despair tumbling across the page. The letter opens, as they would always begin: 'My dearest Meryl'.

*

When I married Hugh, I believed the attention and gifts he showered upon me were an indication of his love. He was thirty. I was eighteen. Too impressionable and naïve to recognise our marriage for what it truly was. A financial merger, the union of two powerful families. I soon came to understand his attention was manipulation. The extremes of generosity, the diamonds, the furs, a method of distracting me and discharging himself from fleeting moments of guilt.

A year after we married I purchased Medley, a house centuries old, built close to Beaumaris on the island of Anglesey. Initially it was to be a weekend retreat for the both of us. Hugh hated it. He despised the ivy-smothered stonework, the hotchpotch of rooms with uneven floors. Gradually his presence at Medley grew less and less. When our third anniversary slipped by unnoticed, I found it was no longer my bolt-hole, a place where I could lick my wounds. It had become my home.

Although living independently of one another, Hugh insisted for two weeks in the year we should appear together in London. It was ridiculous, of course. I recall the first party we'd attended as man and wife, and asking Hugh who the thin, beautiful blonde who had draped herself around him for most of the night was.

"Good grief, Meryl. Can't you guess? She's my mistress." He laughed and kissed me on the cheek. "My dear, you're sweet and so very beautiful, however I'm afraid if you expected fidelity you've chosen the wrong man."

Yet as war loomed I felt it almost my duty, no matter how unpleasant, to be at his side. In August 1939, I travelled down to London to spend a fortnight at his house in Mayfair.

Seven hours after war was declared, after air raid sirens had howled across London and rattlers warned of a gas attack, our car raced to a party in Belgravia.

"You will behave, Meryl?" Hugh said.

The all-clear siren had sounded. The rain was easing. The sky lightening. The streets had begun to fill.

"What on earth are you staring at? Did you hear what I said?"

The sharpness of his voice caused me to turn back in my seat. I glanced across and smiled. "Yes, of course."

"I mean you won't start talking about that bloody house of yours. I overheard the conversation you were having last night. The subject of broken water pipes may be fascinating to you and your chums out in the sticks, but it's hardly scintillating conversation for the First Admiral."

"Was he the First Admiral? Sorry."

The thirty or so guests inside the drawing room turned as the door opened. Women, a blaze of jewellery and silk. Men, their dull coloured uniforms pinned with gleaming brass. Our host broke away from the crowd and hurried over.

"You two cut it fine. We're just about to go into dinner."

Candles flickered along a table. White roses flowed from crystal vases. I was seated between our host and a man wearing the full regalia of a Colonel in the Fusiliers. He eyed me up and down.

"Bailey. How do you do? You must be Hugh's wife?"

"Yes. Hello."

"Saw the red hair and green eyes and thought it must be. Meryl isn't it?"

"Yes."

As the first course was served, conversation around the table briefly touched on the weather: unseasonably warm, wet, the thunderstorms. The recent news of galleries closing. Treasures being crated and shipped away. Money: where should one invest, now war was upon us? How much did one risk? And on what? Steel seemed to be the safest option.

My neighbour, the Colonel, nudged my arm. "Has Hugh mentioned I was instrumental in his company landing the government contract? Jolly glad to do it. Marvellous chap, isn't he? Frightfully ambitious. He's told me all about you. Understand you're from Wales. North or south?"

"North."

"I know the area. Slightly. Have a sister who spends every summer in a town on the coast. Place called Llan… Llandu…"

"Llandudno?"

"That's it! Bloody Welsh names. Can never manage to get my tongue around them."

He took a deep gulp of wine, signalled to a waiter for a refill then twisted around in his seat to face me. Dabbing at the perspiration beading across his flushed, bloated face, he leaned forward and continued in a lower tone. "Wouldn't mind getting my tongue around you, though. Hugh's description didn't do you justice. Seems a shame, beautiful woman like you all alone. Why don't I come over for a weekend? Keep you company?"

I sensed Hugh was watching and instinctively

looked across the table to where he sat. Laughter played on his lips. Yet hidden beneath this smile, I glimpsed something else in the exchange that darted between Bailey and Hugh. It was one of conspiracy.

When dinner was over, hot, tired and miserable, I rose from the table. French doors led out onto a balcony. I stepped outside. With trembling hands, I lit a cigarette and longed for Medley.

"Mind if I join you?"

I turned around to find a man stood in the doorway.

"Please do."

He stood beside me as I stared out across the London rooftops. Music filtered from an open window. The familiar drone of traffic. Horns. Shouts. Normality resuming following the all-clear. Yet sandbags were piled up everywhere. Barrage balloons hovered above.

I smiled as his foot tapped to the beat of the music. "You like Benny Goodman?" I asked.

"The 'King of Swing'? Sure." He offered his hand. "Jack Payne. Originally Vancouver, and now London, England. You?"

"Visiting."

He was tall. Athletic. Sandy hair with a tanned complexion. Handsome. His gaze unsettled me and I found myself babbling, attempting to fill what I sensed was an awkward silence. "I've been here a fortnight.

Home tomorrow. Some shopping after breakfast. A dash to a chocolatier in the Royal Arcade before I catch my train. A box of chocolates. A treat for my housekeeper."

The music stopped and a radio was turned on. "This is the BBC. At 11.15 this morning the British Prime Minister announced . . ."

"Terribly grim, isn't it? Will you remain in Britain now we're at war, Mr. Payne?"

"That's the plan. Been waiting for the politicians to finish what they do. Now the talking's over it's my turn, that's if the RAF will have me."

I sensed Hugh would soon come looking for me. I stubbed out my cigarette and held out my hand. "It's been nice meeting you, Mr. Payne. Goodbye and good luck."

"I'd prefer it if you called me Jack. Goodnight."

I walked away thinking his final comment seemed odd. What chance was there of us meeting again?

Next morning, I woke to find Hugh, always an early riser, had left for work. After my shower I wrote him a letter. I removed my wedding ring, sealed both inside an envelope and left it on his desk in the library. Collecting my handbag and gas mask, I locked the door, pushed the keys through the letter box and walked away. For good.

A taxi dropped me at the corner of Sackville Street. I window-shopped for a while. Attempted to make believe the world was as it should be. Yet it was impossible to avoid the expressions on the faces of passers-by, the fear on upturned faces searching leaden skies. The dazed and tearful children, dragged along by overwrought parents weighed down with suitcases, rushing for evacuation trains and buses. A poster: Hitler will send no warning.

I walked to the Royal Arcade and purchased the chocolates. Before hailing a taxi I paused near the Royal Academy to buy a newspaper. I glanced at the headlines as I waited for my change. When I next looked up, Jack Payne was stood beside me. He seemed out of breath.

"Hi, Meryl. Are you leaving?"

"Jack! How extraordinary! Yes, I should catch the 11.10, if I hurry."

The stall-holder, overhearing my remark, chuckled. "You'll be bloody lucky. Nobody but the kiddies leaving today. Evacuees got priority over everyone."

I bit my lip and pondered the difficulty of finding a hotel room when the city seemed full to bursting.

"I can take you home if you like," Jack said. "I've got a car parked just around the corner."

"I couldn't possibly . . ."

"It's no problem. Where exactly is home?"

I couldn't help but smile. "Wales."

He threw his head back and laughed. "Well, I guess now I've volunteered. Come on."

"At least we can give her a run," he said, holding open the door of a sports car. "See what she's really made of. In you get."

The Morgan - a 4/4 or was it a 4/5? I can never remember - had seen better days. It had a peculiar growl. It had been tweaked, he told me. I had no idea what tweaking was, but it didn't take long before I found out. Once we had left the confines of London, Jack pressed his foot down on the accelerator and the Morgan flew.

Fields and hedgerows passed in a blur. Terrified sheep scattered. Residents of sleepy villages stopped whatever they were doing to watch us fly by. He drove recklessly. Marvellously. In those hours of travelling, we talked more, shared more, laughed more, than I had ever done in three years of marriage to Hugh.

Jack was an electrical engineer. With his business in Canada flourishing, he had expanded and opened more premises in London. He described his childhood. His father's death in the last war.

"I'm sorry."

"No, it's okay. Never knew him. He was killed at Vimy Ridge in 1917, just before I was born." He was quiet for a while. I glanced his way and, though he smiled, I sensed the loss of his father went far deeper than he claimed.

We stopped at a roadside inn. Low beams and a

smoky fire. A few locals perched on stools and chatting at the bar. We found a table in the corner and ordered beer and sandwiches. I was describing the finishing school in Switzerland I'd attended, when the sandwiches - chewy - and the beer - watery – arrived.

"Finishing?" he asked.

I briefly explained. I could see he was struggling to hide his amusement.

"One cannot possibly," I said, mimicking a teacher I'd known and one of the many bizarre opinions she'd held, "be allowed entrance into society until one can produce a Bird of Paradise by the intricate folding of a linen napkin."

He began to laugh and so did I. So much of our conversation would be this way. Total nonsense.

We arrived at Medley long after midnight. I showed him to his room and we said goodnight. I undressed and lay staring up at the ceiling, reliving each moment of the journey. A bird was stirring, light filtering through the curtains, when I rose and tapped on Jack's door.

I recall my embarrassment when he appeared. My sudden fear that my arrival, my willingness, would be misinterpreted. He took my hand and gently pulled me to him. Wrapping his arms around me he whispered, "I think you know our meeting again wasn't down to chance, Mel."

He left the following morning for Bedford. I received

a short letter. It was one full of hope and excitement.

My dearest Meryl,

It's only been three days and you won't believe how much I miss you. Medical and interview was a breeze. I'm in! Basic training delayed so can I visit? Write more later.

All my love. Jack.

He returned to Medley and stayed for three months. We walked hand-in-hand along deserted beaches. Ate sandy picnics under umbrellas. Drank wine, talked, kissed and made love, late into the night. It was as if we both understood time was against us. We talked of marriage. Children. The obstacle preventing us from realising our dream. Hugh continued to ignore my request for a divorce.

I dreaded Jack leaving. If I had known the casualty rate during training for Bomber Command, I doubt I could have borne it. Yet he left. And I did.

Jack was posted to Lincolnshire and began his operational tour flying a Halifax bomber. Each night he set out across the channel, to attack the heavy industry clustered along the Rhine. By the end of June he had completed eight missions and his daily letters remained cheerful.

...Eight hours flying and only a Fry's bar to eat. After debriefing could hardly wait for my bacon and eggs. Won't be long before I'm finished here and can give you a hand with the allotment. Are you still digging for victory? Attagirl! Weather's holding up. Another one down and twenty-two to go! Great news - couple of weeks and I'll have some leave. Only a '48'. Can you come down?...

Optimism, the belief that one day we would once again be together, fuelled our correspondence. Yet the distance between us resulted in hours of travelling. Sometimes, the effort rewarded by just a few hours in a tea-room beside a railway platform.

Since leaving London I'd heard nothing from Hugh. I wrote again repeating the request I'd already made. I wanted a divorce. He replied:

You are my wife. You will remain my wife. Until death.

Jack completed his thirty missions then received news he was being posted back to Canada as an instructor. We didn't see one another until 1944.

I heard the growl of an engine. The crunch of tyres on gravel as the Morgan, driven recklessly, hurtled up the lane and ground to a halt outside the front door. I ran to greet him but before we could embrace he held me at arm's length.

"I've signed on for another twenty."

"What?" I couldn't believe what he'd said.

"I'm doing another twenty."

"No! For God's sake, you can't. You're one of the few who survived thirty. Why on earth would you risk it again? You've been so lucky. And what about me? What about us?" I slapped his hands away.

"It's different. Safer. I'll be flying a Lancaster, we've got long-range fighters, pathfinders to mark our targets. There's gee, oboe, all sorts of navigational systems." He took a step towards me. "We can finish this. Think about it, Mel. What hope is there for us, if we lose this war?"

I could never remain cross for long with Jack. How could I? His confidence in himself and in what he did, this faith each mission would bring us closer to defeating Germany, seemed to rub off on everyone he met. Including me. His new crew welcomed the opportunity to fly with a skipper who had been so lucky.

With the casualty lists growing, the weather deteriorating, seventeen operations scrubbed moments before departure, the nerves of even the most heroic and determined began to shred. Jack wrote, following his fifth sortie:

Remember Mac, our rear gunner? He's no longer with us. Night fighters all over us last night and he cracked. Screaming like a banshee. Awful. There'll be a medical diagnosis but he could be placed LMF - Lacking Moral Fibre. Mac was probably the bravest man in the crew and doing the toughest job of all. This bloody war, it could happen to anyone. All leave cancelled, I'll ring you...

He had once spoken of revenge, relishing the prospect of dropping what was called the 'cookie', the 4,000lb bomb on Hitler's head, and dedicating the act to his father. He wrote:

We targeted the 'big city' last night. Berlin. PFF arrived late so we were left circling the target under colossal flak. Bloody nightmare. No thought of dad and revenge as the cookie dropped. Just wanted to turn our kite around and get home in one piece. Anyway, another one over. Please God it won't be too long before I see you again. I love you so much. Keep safe. Jack.

It was as if he sensed his luck was running out.

Three days later Jack was posted missing. A pilot, a friend of Jack's, rang me. He described what happened.

"We were on a raid. Attacking a munitions factory

near Stuttgart. Searchlights locked onto Jack's plane. He tried to fly his way out of it, used some tremendous manoeuvres, but the guns had their target. He managed to stay with the returning stream until we crossed into France, then his plane began losing altitude. My navigator counted six 'chutes, so Jack was probably still struggling with the controls as his crew bailed out. Well Jack would, wouldn't he? He's that sort of chap. Very brave."

He was missing, he wasn't dead. I repeated the words over and over in my mind as I worked in the garden from dawn to dusk. I dug, hacked, clawed at weeds and brambles in the allotment until my hands bled. I concealed my grief. To reveal it to others would have been the first step in admitting Jack was dead. And I refused to give up hope.

Hugh appeared a few weeks later. We stood facing one another in the hall. He had changed. Aged. The late nights, the parties, the heavy drinking had overtaken his looks. He was pale, lined, a puffiness around his bloodshot eyes. He bore all the signs of a man who had lived too well. Or so I thought.

"I was worried about you, Meryl," he said. "Dilys told me about your friend. I'm very sorry."

"Jack. His name's Jack and he's not dead. He's missing. He'll come back."

"Yes...yes, of course. Sorry to turn up like this, I

was wondering if I could stay? I've got a pile of work to get through and needed some peace and quiet. It'll just be for a few weeks or so. Promise I won't be a bother and, I thought, if you still want to, maybe we could discuss the divorce?"

I glanced down at the luggage scattered across the floor. Suitcases, boxes, his briefcase. It seemed the decision had already been made. I shrugged. "I'll ask Dilys to prepare a room."

Hugh lived with me at Medley for three months. Most mornings, long before I had risen, he would have breakfasted and retreated to the study. He always seemed to have an excuse whenever I raised the subject of divorce.

Never a patient man, as the weeks passed he became even more petulant. He cursed the draughts and the chilliness of Medley. He complained of the unnecessary trips to the hall to answer the telephone. A fire was lit each morning and a telephone extension fitted in the study. This need to argue and rage against anything and everything escalated. When one day I found Dilys sobbing in the kitchen, I decided I'd had enough.

The curtains drawn, a solitary lamp cast a paltry glow in the study. A log fire burnt in the hearth. Hugh, his head in his hands when I had stormed in, looked up and gestured to an ink pot which had spilt across a muddle of books and papers on the desk.

"Look! Look what she's done. Stupid, bloody woman. I want her gone. Do you understand? Sacked. Today. This instant."

I stared at him. For the first time I noticed how much weight he had lost. How his shirt collar drooped untidily at his neck. How his skin bore a yellowish tinge.

"Hugh! Are you ill? You look dreadful. What on earth's the matter?"

Wincing with pain and using his desk for support he sank into a chair. "I've got cancer, Meryl. Pretty bad it seems. Disease is spreading faster than the docs anticipated. Bloody nuisance."

"Why didn't you tell me? Is this the reason you've come back?" I sat down in the chair opposite him. "You're working too hard, Hugh. You must send this." I thumbed through the papers littering his desktop. "All of this must go back to London. You need to rest."

"Rest?" He shook his head. "Not yet, Meryl. Not quite yet."

I found a camp bed stored away in the attic and placed it in the study. He remained there, working, reading, speaking on the telephone, until the day after my birthday when he asked to be taken upstairs to his room.

Between us, Dilys and I nursed him. In those final days I sat beside his bed as he drifted in and out of consciousness. Not long before he died, he opened his eyes. He gestured to the bedside table. I opened a drawer and, reaching inside, I withdrew two letters and glanced back to Hugh.

The dullness clouding his eyes for so many weeks had vanished. In its place glowed a momentary and hideous flame of triumph as he said, "Read them. Read them and remember."

The first letter was from a nursing sister at a hospital in Berkshire.

Dear Mrs. Hamilton,

Mr. Jack Payne is unable to write and has asked me to do so on his behalf. After bailing out of his aircraft, Jack was sheltered and nursed, at considerable risk to themselves, by a French farmer and his family. He had multiple injuries, the most severe being burns, mainly to his legs and hands. When Allied troops broke through German lines he was transferred to this hospital. Given time we believe he will make a full recovery and this recovery will be greatly assisted if you should visit.

K. Holdsworth. SRN

I opened the second letter dated a month after the

first.

My dearest Meryl,

I realise now you must have been pretty mad at me for going back. Guess I didn't appreciate how much. I'm sorry I messed up. Have you met someone else? I'm told they'll be shipping me back to Canada soon. Perhaps I shouldn't press but I'd like to talk to you. One last time. I'll ring on the 14th. At least I can wish you a happy birthday.

All my love,

Jack.

    I folded the letters and returned them to their envelopes.
    I looked back at Hugh. His eyes remained open. Dull. Lifeless.
    You are my wife. You will remain my wife. Until death.

*

Oystercatchers feeding on the shoreline call out as the sun sinks to an orange glow. I close the lid of the box, breathe in the cold salty air and think of him. I rang the hospital on the day Hugh died. They refused to give me any information. I have written a letter, begging them to forward it onto Jack. There has been no reply and I cannot help but feel his silence is my answer. I have lost him.

The shadows are lengthening. I climb to my feet, pull my coat around me and begin retracing my steps up the bank.

The steep climb is a struggle. As I pause to catch my breath I hear something. It is a noise quite far in the distance yet growing louder. I begin to climb again and, in my haste, slip several times before I reach the top of the bank. The oystercatchers hear it too; they shriek with annoyance and take flight.

My breath comes in short gasps. I begin to run as I recognise the noise for what it is. A car. A Morgan. Driven recklessly.

Diamonds And Rust
Carole Pitt

"I wish you were coming with us."

Ginny squeezed the small hand reassuringly. "I have to stay home, sweetheart, I've got jobs to do for Grandma. Anyway, Daddy is looking forward to taking you on holiday."

She bent down to wipe away the tears from the small face.

"Are you ready to go now?"

Emma nodded.

Out on the drive, Ginny watched her eldest daughter, Beth, adding to the heap of luggage.

"This is way too many bags for a week in Cornwall," Clive said.

"It's called covering every eventuality," Ginny explained.

"Notice how they avoid putting them in the boot."

"Try asking them nicely, it might work."

It was late July and the first week of the school holidays. The day promised a taste of the heat-wave that was to come, but Ginny felt cold in the early morning sunshine.

"Hey, you okay?" Clive asked.

"Of course I am. I guess it's the prospect of dealing with Ma. If only she had stayed with us instead of her barmy mate; it adds an extra ten miles to my journey. One final moan before you go. Not too many ice creams, or candy floss and burgers."

"If you want to monitor my parental skills, go and pack," he replied.

"I'm only joking," she said wrapping her arms around him. She leaned her head against his chest. "You, my love, are everything that's good and sparkling in my life."

Clive brushed his hand gently across her cheek. "And you are the best thing that ever happened to me."

"I almost forgot." Ginny suddenly let go and looked up at her husband. "Shall I open your letter if it comes?"

"It can wait until I get back. I don't need any more distractions other than those two." He turned and watched Emma and Beth climb into the car. "It seems we're finally ready to hit the road."

Ginny gave him a brief hug and waited while he checked the girl's seatbelts.

"See you next Friday," he yelled.

She watched until the car turned left onto the main road.

Ginny's heart thumped erratically. She prayed he'd remembered everything. At work, her husband was the most organised person she'd ever known. At home, the total opposite. If she challenged him on the subject, his response was always the same. Most of his colleagues turned into slobs at home. Ordered minds, he clarified, often switched to being disordered. It was an occupational hazard.

There was a fifty percent chance of them turning around. She would wait in the garden. Going indoors could be risky.

It had started two months earlier. Carla had insisted they spend a day shopping in London. Later, when they got back to Paddington station, she had spotted him walking towards the exit to the underground. She had stood rooted to the spot, convinced she was mistaken. But he too stopped and stared. There had been no acknowledgment, he just stood watching and waiting.

Once she was on the train, her legs had begun to shake. The carriage filled rapidly, and Carla nowhere in sight. With claustrophobia adding to her panic, she had shoved her way through the crowded aisles towards the buffet. Carla was at the front of the queue about to be served.

"Shopping makes me thirsty," Carla said, handing Ginny a miniature bottle of vodka and a can of tonic. The nearest seats were in the quiet zone. They had talked all day and Ginny was relieved when Carla dozed off. For the duration of the journey, Ginny remembered the past.

*

It had been ten years. One night he had walked out and never returned. Afterwards, there was always the fear he would get in touch. A communication of some sort, but there had been none. No phone calls, no email, nothing. No one had heard of or seen him in the intervening years. Gradually people stopped talking about him. Ginny had moved two hundred miles south and started a new life. It had taken a long time to recover, and now a chance sighting could ruin everything.

*

Ginny drove to her mother's bungalow. This was the third time she'd checked and still no sign of any workers. After six weeks and with no sign of a completion date, Ginny was angry. She let herself in and was horrified to see the state of the place. None of the builders had bothered to tidy up. A porcelain figurine lay in pieces on the hearth. Ginny picked them up and threw them into the bin, knowing she would be held responsible. Now she would have to find a replacement, which would not be cheap.

The best solution was to threaten the builders, imply there would be no final payment if the conservatory remained unfinished. Her anger and frustration eventually impressed the receptionist. She suggested she call round and speak to the manager personally. The combination of heat and another confrontation made her feel sick. Once the manager realised she meant business he answered every question, apologised several times and said the work would definitely resume this Friday.

Sorting out her mother's affairs had briefly helped to forget about the first phone call. But the urge to confide in someone was getting stronger. After leaving the building company, she found herself driving round in circles.

As she parked outside Carla's small Victorian house the temperature was hovering close to eighty-five degrees. Her cotton sun-dress had turned into a limp rag, and her dark hair was damp with sweat. Carla, of Mediterranean descent, seemed unaffected by the heat and was toiling away on her patio.

"You must be mad gardening on a day like today," Ginny shouted above the radio.

Carla had her hands in a grow bag, planting small brightly coloured geraniums.

"Well hello," she said. "How does it feel to be a free agent?"

"Not as wonderful as I imagined."

"So the handsome bloke I saw you with outside Waitrose is married, too."

Ginny knew she had been stupid talking to him in a public place. Carla's expression was unreadable.

"I must admit I'm stunned. You don't strike me as the type to have an affair, and why didn't you tell me?"

Ginny sat down.

Carla carried on. "You look a tad pensive. Regretting it already?"

"Do you remember the last time we went to London?"

"Oh, two or three months back, when I bought those wonderful red patent shoes. The ones I can't wear because they cripple me. How could I possibly forget?"

"I saw someone that day, someone from my past."

"And I take it there lies the problem?" Carla said.

"Yes, a big problem."

"And you've come here to talk about it."

"I'm not sure what to do. He's an old boyfriend I haven't seen for ten years. There have been phone calls and now he's following me."

"I presume you haven't told Clive."

"No way, I can't tell Clive, but one thing I am not doing is cheating on my husband." Carla held up her hand, a gesture Ginny knew to obey. "Let me open a bottle of wine before you say any more."

Ginny wasn't about to tell the whole story. The persona she created after moving south was not the real

Ginny. She was fully aware Carla thought of her as an unassuming housewife with little ambition. When Carla returned with the drinks she came straight to the point.

"Okay, if he's not screwing you then it has to be blackmail. And the reason why, you are not going to tell me."

"I can't tell you. One day you and I might fall out."

"So you don't trust me?"

Ginny nodded.

"Okay, I'm a lawyer, but not your lawyer, so I understand. How much does he want for not exposing your nasty secret to Clive?"

"Fifty thousand."

Carla took a big gulp of wine. "Jesus, Ginny, what did you do?"

Ginny rarely drank during the day and the combination of hot sun and wine had made her feel strange. "I think I'd better go home, it's getting late."

Carla poured more wine. "I don't have go to work tomorrow. Stay here for a couple of days and sleep on it. I have various ideas for a solution. A few of which don't involve a fifty grand payout."

For the first time since she moved in Ginny was afraid to unlock the front door. The house appeared forbidding. Almost as if a loathsome presence inhabited the interior, one that had decided to stay.

A warm south-westerly wind rustled the beech trees lining the drive, the branches casting shadows across the pale walls. The moonlight changed the windows to mirrors; the reflections of the branches reaching out, mocking her. Ginny's hand trembled as she inserted the key into the lock.

She had been so proud of her home, a five-bedroom Georgian terrace she had painstakingly renovated. Not once had she felt guilty about how she came by it, until now. Her mind recalled the very first phone conversation.

*

"I'd like to see you again."

"That's impossible. You disappear off the face of the earth, then ten years later turn up and act as if nothing happened."

"I've never stopped thinking about you. We were good together and we could be again."

"You know I'm married now with a family."

"I do. I've seen your handsome husband and pretty little girls."

Ginny took a deep breath. "I won't deceive my husband."

"We can be discreet."

It had been stupid to dismiss his real reasons for contacting her. Looking back, she had been naïve to think he intended to relinquish his share of the money forever. At the time, guilt may have driven him away, after what he had done to her. Rape, even between lovers and proved beyond reasonable doubt, carried a hefty sentence. Those ten years had been sufficient for him to feel safe from prosecution.

In the darkness she made her way to bed. Sleep evaded her until dawn. When she woke, the phone was ringing. Today was the deadline.

Ginny let it ring, trying to curb the fear. Meeting in a public place was out of the question, and there was no way she could have him in her home. When she picked up she had the solution.

"Do you remember where my mother lives?"

"Somewhere near the Greystone estate. So she's still around then, the old doll."

"Yes she is, but staying with a friend at the moment. We can meet there if you like. I can't have you here."

"That's a shame," he said.

"It's better to be out of sight."

"I'm still disappointed." He waited a second. "Next time I can treat you to a fancy hotel room."

Ginny tried to control her voice. "The bungalow is the last one on Stepping Stone Lane, before you meet the crossroads."

"I'll see you there then, early evening. You managed to raise all of it, then. I'm impressed."

Meeting at her Mother's house had not been part of his plan. A very public place was what he had wanted, to compromise her further and gain control. She knew even when he got what he came for it would never be over. Then he would have time to concentrate on his needs.

Ginny had no desire to become another statistic. Perhaps she was being paranoid; if so it was no surprise, considering the history. She drained the glass of wine and poured another. As the alcohol relaxed her she began to see that appealing to his better nature was the way to go. That she could not see him again, that she adored her husband and children. That their relationship had been a nightmare and there would be no re-igniting it. Before she fell back into an uneasy sleep, Ginny offered a silent prayer that he would disappear again just as he had ten years before.

They wouldn't be able to use the kitchen, so Ginny moved the old Formica table into the sitting room. She placed a bottle of wine and two glasses in the centre.

The evening was unbearably humid; she wandered into the garden and looked at the view. Growing up in the house, she'd hated the isolation. Tonight she was glad of it; no one should see him arrive.

Her fingers trembled when she opened the door; the ten years had been kind to him. The amazing blue eyes and the cultivated arrogance were still there. She forced a smile to hide the disgust and hatred.

"I've thought about this day for years," he said.

"I don't want to talk about the past," Ginny replied. "I'd rather talk about now. How long are you back for?"

"I guess that will depend on you."

She wondered about his relatives. "How's your family?"

"Well, that's an interesting question. Let's say I don't have any contact with them."

"All those years we were together and I knew so little about you," Ginny said.

"There was nothing to know, I was a loner and I'm still a loner."

"I can't see you after tonight," Ginny said quietly. I'm happy with my life now, and you were cruel and controlling. I could never ever go back to such a destructive relationship." He pulled her into an embrace. "I've changed and if you give me another chance, I'll make it up to you."

He seemed so confident and laid-back. As if they were just catching up and the years were of little consequence. She watched him carefully, the alcohol and its inevitable effect, turning back to the horrible creature she'd known so intimately.

Ginny shook him off. "Can I tell you something?" she said. "You could never make it up to me and you're mad to assume I could care for someone so vile."

"That's not a very nice thing to say, considering you killed a defenceless old woman. How you persuaded the cops it was an assisted suicide is beyond me. If it hadn't been for your fancy friends helping you to lie...At least you kept your promise and didn't implicate me."

Ginny's rage escalated. "She asked me to help her. The only mistake I made was telling you."

He lit a cigarette and smiled. "People get away scot-free now. I always wondered when murder would be legalised."

"Don't forget, you bastard, how you pressured me. I was besotted with you. I've paid for it ever since and I don't intend to carry on living in fear. Right now, I'd like you to leave and if you ever contact me again you will find I'm not as scared of you as I was all those years ago."

She got up to clear away the dishes and he caught her by the wrist.

"Money first, then come and sit on my knee."

She shook his hand away; there was a familiar look in the blue eyes, his word was still a command.

"Leave me alone, never ever touch me again."

"I don't think so," he said.

Suddenly she was encompassed by strong arms. She felt his hand move to her breast and she pushed him away.

"Don't you ever dare do that to me again."

He tried to pick her up and Ginny stifled the scream. She must not cry out, whatever he did. The grip on her body tightened and his expression was manic.

"If you don't do this voluntarily, I'll make you."

Ginny struggled furiously, thinking this can't be happening again. Please God, not again. He stopped trying to pick her up and instead slammed her hard to the ground next to the small table. She hung on to the leg and felt it move. A wine goblet placed too close to the edge fell and shattered. As he fumbled with the buttons on her dress, her hand closed on a fragment of the glass. It sliced deep into her palm as her grip tightened. Slowly she moved her free arm; the other was pinned down by his weight. There would be only one chance. She raised her hand and when he lifted his head to look into her eyes she plunged it into his neck.

"You bitch," he said.

He tried tugging at the glass, but he was weakening. Ginny watched as he slumped away, freeing her. Then she examined her hand; it was bleeding badly. /

won't need stitches, she decided. *Because there is no way I can go to the hospital.* Then she waited.

The conservatory was still a basic carcass of three walls and roof. The builders had covered the empty window-frames with a thick tarpaulin. She looked down at the floor; it too was covered with heavy black plastic sheeting, anchored down by bricks on each corner. Which corner to pull away? Underneath she saw the layer of hardcore and digging seemed an impossible task. But there was sufficient time; it wouldn't be light until five. Ginny made her way to the bottom of the garden and noticed the builders had left two bags of lime, she supposed for rendering. She knew what she had to do with it. If they asked where it had gone she would say some local had probably pinched it.

It took her three hours to dig deep enough to conceal the body. Fortunately she didn't have far to drag it. She tipped the lime over him as if she was accustomed to the task. Then she examined the floor, checking for any ripple of unevenness, any evidence of what lay beneath. There was no time to lose; after the lecture she had delivered to the builders, she knew they would be here promptly to deliver the ready-mix. Concrete, her memory jerked around in her head. What had she read recently to do with dogs? She felt a sudden surge of panic. The article was about cadaver dogs. They had been used on a high-profile case, and had detected human remains beneath several feet of cement. Ginny went through her family members one by one, trying to remember if any of them had a dog. She calmed down; no one had one. These specialist dogs took years to train. Also, she reassured herself, by the time the workmen had trampled all over the place, she was confident that there would be little evidence of anything. They could have their tea breaks in the sitting room, then any DNA would be a melting pot, not easy to separate, even with the low copy number science. She would allow herself half an hour to rest. The site manager assured her the concrete wouldn't take more than a few hours to harden, especially in the present heat. He had advised her not to walk on it for two or three days. Then he would personally arrange for one of his guys to lay the garish ceramic tiles her Mother had chosen. After that, completion would be within the two weeks she'd specified.

There was only one thing left she must do.

Carla was full of ideas.

"It's okay; he's decided to go back to Canada. Panic over." Ginny concentrated on her light-hearted tone.

"Am I glad to hear that," Carla said.

*

The heat wave finally broke the last night of the holiday. Clive didn't relish the two hundred mile journey home. He dreaded the M5; it would be a nightmare in torrential rain and thunderstorms. According to the early weather forecast, the South West, stretching from Birmingham to Truro, was at risk of flooding. He hoped Ginny wasn't planning on driving anywhere. He'd missed her and couldn't wait to be home.

Clive opened the front door with his key; the girls got soaked from running the short distance from the car.

"Go and get changed straight away, you two," he ordered.

"Mummy, Mummy, we're back. Where are you, Mummy?"

"She's probably gone to the shops. I didn't ring to say we were leaving earlier, because of the weather."

Clive noticed the house was spotless. There were flowers on the kitchen table, and a plain white envelope with his name on. The handwriting was Ginny's.

"Can I watch telly?" asked Beth.

"Did you miss it on holiday?"

"No, but I miss it now."

"Okay then. Mum's bound to be back soon."

He opened the letter, relieved at the content. Then he went looking for his wife. From the kitchen window he watched as she locked the garden shed.

"Hi, I thought you'd gone out." He kissed her and held up the letter. "What happened to the original envelope?"

"Sorry, I cut myself on the old secateurs." She held up the bandaged hand. "I couldn't let you open a blood-stained letter, certainly not one so important."

She smiled; some of the stress he'd noticed over the previous weeks had vanished. She put her arms around his neck and whispered. "Congratulations, Detective Superintendent."

"I think the last few months must have swung in my favour," he said.

"Girls, come here," Ginny shouted. "Daddy's got his promotion."

There was no reply. Emma was engrossed in *Charlie and Lola* and Beth was upstairs.

"You did so well. I'm so proud of you."

"I can't take all the credit. I had a great team and they worked their arses off for me."

"But you had all the brains and you were the one who pulled it together. You put those evil people behind bars for the rest of their lives."

"I got lucky," he said and pulled her close. "Besides, we all know there is no such thing as the perfect crime."

The Only Conclusion
Daniel Lewis

We slide onto the single bed and I lose myself in her green million mile eyes. We hear them mounting stairs, but don't panic, because I am king and she is queen and we are together.

It's hotter than I've ever known it to be. My heart sighs as I lick the sweat from her lips then smile as she smiles. I feel the oddest excitement. She draws her arm around me, and we kiss as they enter the bedroom.

Their hands are gentler than expected as they pull us apart. Earlier, they'd called us animals, but they call us nothing now; they know we've brought the worst punishment upon ourselves. They lead us separately from the room, all using one hand to restrain us, one hand to wipe their brows. And then we are apart. Cracked in two, for the first and last time.

I'm alone in my cell, yet still see her, feel her inside me. I see through those green million miles how everything ends, and how it all begins.

*

It wasn't always this hot. But, still, the first thing I remember is sitting in that sandpit, back burning, staring at her as grains filtered like ants between my fingers.

"I had only just moved to the town…I was doomed from the start," she joked years later. "You saw me first, and ripped away any chance of a quiet life."

They say that you can't fall in love at the age of three, can't map your life's course before your mind comprehends all options. But they know nothing of love. If they did, they'd have let us be. And we'd have let them live.

I didn't talk to her that day, but I got her attention: every time I whipped off my T-shirt, Mrs. Waite forced it back on me. I allowed her to supervise me a few times, then threw the sweat-soaked shirt at her. And, as I was lifted sand-kicking from the pit and smacked, my eyes locked with the new girl's.

We spoke the following day, and from then on were inseparable. There's no point rationalising what drew me to her; we were too young for our needs to be physical, and it took time to learn her character. But, like her, I was an only child; perhaps we chose to be together because we shared that aching desire to not quite be alone. Or perhaps it was something more instinctual. Primal.

Our union unnerved the teachers, yet their fears paled besides our parents'. Initially pleased with the friendship, they grew cautious, concerned, as the intensity of our relationship became clear. Our actions would be easier to justify if our parents had been deviants, hiding urges behind a suburban sheen. But we were born into good families, lacking money yet never affection or security.

I think that's how things were, anyway. It's difficult to remember, because that day, when we were seven years old, distorts all prior memories.

I'm not ignorant. I read the news. They delighted in lumping that accident in with our list of crimes; they grew hysterical, told the world the first blood we spilt was the thickest, and added another four to our admittedly lengthy tally. Yet they painted us in crude strokes. Yes, there were cross words in that car, but the first deaths she and I witnessed were not at our hands. And, though I lament what occurred, if we hadn't staggered from bushes and fire to find each other that day, then perhaps we wouldn't have led this beautiful life.

I…I can remember. The sky was as purple, yellow, orange as the bodies I'd disentangled myself from. I saw she and she saw me. We stood and stared at perfect mirror images: bloody and blooded, weeping as much with relief as loss. Dying sun rays highlighted her long hair and mine. I moved towards my twin, took her hand, and we ran.

We ran and never stopped.

I'm not sure what else we could have done. We

were seven, and suddenly only had each other. We grew feral, yet developed our wits and educated each other. We stole books and learned to read, calculate, understand maps…and valued those texts as much as the food we salvaged from bins, as the piss-stained mattresses we dragged to our lair.

We survived, we grew, we spoke to no one but each other.

They'd love you to believe that it was simply bloodlust that drove us on; after all, we are the ultimate public enemies. You hate us, you fear us, a sliver of you wants to be who you believe we are. But we never sought out violence. We survived three trouble-free years because we hid away from life, permanently dirt-streaked phantoms. Until life found us, and inexplicably wished us harm.

I remember killing my first man.

I remember the effortless way his skin slit and parted, remember thinking how little strength and power has to do with taking another's life. I remember his cry, as high as the deer we'd hunted, and less dignified.

We'd separated to scavenge; our nightly routine. I'd found enough bread outside a store to feed us for days, and run back to where I knew she'd be.

Backed against a wet, waste-green wall, her hair near-covered her face but her teeth were bared, imitating that last instinctual rush of fury we'd often provoked in doomed animals. The man's back was to me. His belt buckle clinked as it hit the ground. He moved slowly but I moved fast.

I had to jump to reach his neck. The broken bottle went in at a lucky angle, and his legs buckled comically as he fell. We hadn't seen human blood for three years, but it now hissed at us, fountaining over him before finding its dying rhythm.

Heart thumping in my ears, I stepped over the man and gripped her towards me. We watched him weakly jolt, and I didn't question what I'd done. She was all I knew, and he'd come to harm her. And, though our minds developed as the years flashed by, such instincts never died.

We ran from the alley, through deserted streets we were suddenly warier of, towards our hideaway, chewing bread all the while.

And, when we finally sank to the ground, exhausted yet adrenalised, we became one. We were barely formed, wrestling each other from bloody clothes, yet it felt inevitable. We had no idea what we were doing. I ached so much I thought I was dying. She cried and I panicked until I realised she was happy, and then we slept as we'd never slept before.

We were lovers, and that was that. Only ten,

guessing at life. But, even then, I knew what I still know now: that I would never touch another apart from her. And she, she would always be true to me.

*

I am aware that, despite our loving natures, we sound like animals: vicious, relentless, incapable of mercy. My killing in that alleyway was, as you know, the first of many. And, sitting in my cell, so hot it hurts to inhale, I recount that murder as it marked the moment we became adults. All we ever wished for was to be left alone to celebrate each other. We didn't plan to take the lives of others but, when we had to act, we never hesitated. To kill meant little to us; as long as we were safe and together, we would do whatever we needed to do. Unfortunately, as I'm sure you've read, there were occasional complications. A family died because the eldest son decided to be a hero. A group of friends were buried in a park thanks to their ringleader's callous actions. I'm not proud of those killings, yet must make clear that we never had a choice. Freedom is – was – everything to us, and we could therefore never afford to leave traces of ourselves behind, regardless of the pleas the doomed felt compelled to make.

*

Our lives were filled with joy, and we saw the positive in everything. Most people complained when the rain no longer came, but we – still children, after all – enjoyed our endless summer. I'd inhale that heat as her sweat-slick skin made me dizzy, dive into those green eyes and desire nothing else.

We stole a car when we were sixteen and moved from town to town, careful not to attract attention. Now, they talk of us as blood-crazed teens who suddenly materialised and tallied up over fifty kills. But we'd been us, doing what we did, for many years. Like taking another's life, anonymity is child's play if approached a certain way.

She loved the sea, so we drove to the beach almost every day. People could no longer deal with the water's heat or the lack of shade, so it was usually deserted. We always chose a secluded spot, though, just to be certain.

Whoever it was who left their keys in that car's ignition appreciated their music. Before seizing the car, we only knew music as saccharine snippets heard over the tannoy as we robbed stores, or as a tool for learning in hazily-remembered school days. But this car came with dozens of tapes: in the glove compartment, on the floor, down the backs of seats, and we experienced some of our happiest times as we drove down deserted roads, discovered songs by artists we'd barely heard of and watched the sun mercifully begin its brief descent.

This inherited collection soundtracked our

existence; life was she, me and music. We found songs of rebellion, of pride and fury, heard primal drums and raging guitars, and educated ourselves as best we could. We cherished one song above all others, and played it so often that the tape warped; an effect that oddly complemented its sound. She loved the tune so much it could drive her to tears and, thinking about it now, one of the only times we argued was over the song she'd tattooed onto her heart…

"I want the sea to come to me," she said.

She was lying on me, staring at the bleaching sky as '"Heroes"' swirled from the car parked nearby.

I laughed. "No one can control the sea. Not even you."

"It's not about control. I want us to be submerged as we lie here, so we can hear this song as it was meant to be heard. Because those guitars…that's how dolphins sound."

"Dolphins don't make a sound," I said. "They no longer exist."

She turned to me, her elbow just missing my groin, and I saw sadness in her eyes. "You don't know that for sure."

I stroked her arm, fingers tracing sandy wet hairs. "I know what you've told me."

'"Heroes"' continued at ear-aching volume; David

Bowie's voice surged and grew anxious. Urgent.

"This song is about us, for us," she said. "No one else exists but the one he loves."

It was true. On every other song on the compilation, Bowie sounded like an actor. But, here, he seemed to really be singing to the one he'd chosen to be his heroine.

Then again, for all '"Heroes"' apparent sincerity, its title on the cassette was, unlike other songs, surrounded by quotation marks. And I often wondered: was Bowie being ironic, mocking his heroes' delusions? Was the song a fiction, full of false feeling? Or did he simply consider the couple doomed?

She often complained that my concerns were irrelevant, but I wanted to know the truth before I committed to the song the way she had.

That's why I replied: "And do you *believe* him?"

She jammed her hand against my groin and sprang up. "Don't you dare mention those fucking inverted commas," she hissed, and ran towards the too-warm sea.

I didn't see her for an hour. I lay on the bonnet of the car, metal near burning my skin, but rose every six minutes to rewind the song. And by the time she returned, I'd decided she was right, and put my faith in every word I heard.

*

It's important for her to believe that we too are heroes.

She's in her cell now, staring through her one little window, watching the sun and knowing its intentions. She's thinking about everything we've done and telling herself that we acted for the greater good. She has to; it's the only way she can rationalise what she knows.

She's known all along, thanks to nightmares, visions, and a feeling as firm as the beat of her heart. No, not a feeling. A certainty.

Months after my first outburst, we were together again in the sandpit. Four years old and already soulmates. My top was off, and none of the teachers had the energy to control me. The sun, as usual, pulsed viciously in the sky.

"You'll burn," she said as she tried to sculpt castles.

"I won't. I like the sun…and so do you." I held my milky coffee arm against hers. "See. We're the same."

She smiled, looked older than she was. "But one day you'll burn. And so will I."

Her instinct grew stronger all the time. She calmly told her parents what she knew, but they ignored her, and soon after she was alone with me. She didn't mention it again until I killed that man.

"One day you'll burn," she reminded me. "And so will I. Don't feel guilty about that man. If you hadn't killed him, the sun would have."

As she spoke, I dove into eyes a million miles

deep. I felt warmth – not heat – and knew I had nothing to fear.

Every killing was necessary; neither of us could allow our freedom to be compromised. And the knowledge that we were doing these souls a favour made our decision easier, every single time. A bullet from me or she was quicker, more merciful, than what we will all soon experience.

*

It's nearly time.

Midnight and the sun is still in the sky.

We're the most notorious eighteen-year-olds this town has ever known, yet we've been forgotten. No one has checked in on me in hours, but I can hear commotion in the distance, full of fear of the unknown. I'm dehydrated, but the light-headedness adds to the sense of peace I feel.

We were only supposed to be held here temporarily, but this is now where we'll remain. She is close to me, and yet we haven't once called out to each other. We don't need to.

We could have faced our end back in that bedroom. Though a year ago you'd barely heard of us, we long ago lost all hope of anonymity. The more people knew of our crimes, the more we were hunted, the more we defended ourselves. It was only a matter of time before we were caught. And I'm sure the police who apprehended us have been commended, but they found us because we allowed them to. We broke into the house, chose a bedroom, and waited. There was no point in evading them; her eyes made clear that everything would soon be over. Plus we were tired; it's difficult to run for your life in this heat. So, after years of doing everything to ensure our freedom, we allowed them to capture us, because…well, we're curious. We've known what no one else knows for a while now. And, though our last moments, from flesh to bone to ash, will be painful, we simply wouldn't miss this main event for the world.

We've said our goodbyes. We're at peace, with our actions and their repercussions. And now…now, truth be told, I'm pretty fucking excited.

I'm so excited I can barely breathe. My clothes lie bundled in a corner. I caress the wall, hoping it'll cool me, but it's no help; I'm parched and my heart is thudding violently. I feel fantastic.

I recall what she so often said to me, whenever remorse threatened to trip us up: though we caused pain, we offered salvation. Then again, we also ripped away our victims' opportunity to experience what we now desperately await. So, though I envy their easy escape, I still salute those who met yet never survived us: Meyer Jenkins, the Philips twins, Naomi, Wanda, Big Pat, Little

Pat, the Soursberg family and Fangs, Mrs. Waite, Hattie, Leonard, Liam, Leopold, Suzie O, the Wilsons and their nephew Pete, Hogg Stencil, Flora, Finn, Lewis, Yoyo Temper…plus those we barely knew: the men, women and children who made bad choices and had worse luck, right back to and including the man down the alley who showed me how easy a life like this could be. I hope their rest is peaceful…and, if we meet again, advise them to forget what's done and make the most of what comes next.

Of what comes now.

How I love my girl. She's right, of course. We beat them, forever and ever. From my window, I watch our distant sea bubble and froth and mimic the orangest sky. My eyes burn. I hear screams, but don't make a sound. Layers of life crumble away. I walk through the final divide and, for all the light around us, it's only green I now see. We kiss and, as my queen melts into me, she once again sets my world on fire.

Interception
Tom Singleton

i.

The small jet crossed the Brazilian coast just south of Porto Alegre and began to climb fast as it headed east over the South Atlantic.

At the stipulated time, the Montevideo agent picked up the telephone and called the British consulate. He was put through to the duty intelligence officer. By now the aircraft was clear of Brazilian airspace and flying at 38,000 feet towards its destination, a small landing strip in the countryside north of Bitterfontein in South Africa.

It landed safely and two tall Europeans, helping a stooped old man who looked sick in the sun, descended the steps. They got into a large black Mercedes which set off at high speed.

ii.

The telephone rang and was answered by the night duty officer. He listened to the caller and then asked, "Are you sure?"

"Yes," the caller replied. "I know it's an old protocol but it has never been withdrawn and my system shows it is still active. The passwords that we received fit it exactly."

"But he must be so old by now. The whole world thought he was dead. How can this be happening?"

"I have no idea. Maybe he really is the devil in disguise!"

"So, where is he heading?"

"South Africa, then a regular BA flight from Cape Town to London. That's all I've got."

"OK," said the night duty officer. "Good night."

He terminated the call and typed the password given him into the computer. The response took him by surprise. 'NO ONLINE PROCESS TO FOLLOW. CONTACT PM OFFICE AT ONCE.' So it was not a hoax. It was not the diplomat's little practical joke. This was still current and was something that had been anticipated. He put the call into Downing Street.

iii.

During the time of apartheid and sanctions, South Africa had established very close economic and military links with Israel.

Both countries had felt beleaguered on all sides. Both countries shared some feeling of divine right in their attitude and treatment of the people who had been dispossessed: the majority black population in South

Africa and the Palestinian Arabs in Israel.

Even now, after the release of Mandela, the triumph of the African National Congress and the peaceful establishment of majority rule in South Africa, there were still senior officials in the government and military who shared intelligence with Israel. This was why, across Israel, air force bases were at high security and aircraft were being brought into a state of war readiness.

The briefing officer began to speak. The man behind him, in an open-necked, short-sleeved shirt and dark glasses, remained silent. There were three pilots in the room, the best and most experienced in the intercept wing.

"This is a priority one target of the utmost significance to Israel and to Jewish people around the world. The Americans have not been advised of our plans and you may expect a hostile response from British elements."

The men had been listening carefully but this last comment brought puzzled looks to their faces.

The briefing officer continued. "I am authorised to tell you to intercept a scheduled British Airways flight from Cape Town. It is a 747-400 and has just taken off with all seats full. Due to your operational limitations it will not be possible to order it to change course and escort it back here. You must therefore destroy it in the air, probably in

Tunisian air space."

The officer paused. The aircrew did not speak. They asked no questions. They did not doubt the integrity of the mission, or their ability to carry it out.

"You will be operating through the airspace of several hostile countries and our actions will be deemed aggressive. Air-to-air fuelling will not be possible and you will be operating at maximum range. Hit the target and then ditch at the given co-ordinates. You will be picked up. Any questions so far?"

"Yes," asked the senior pilot present. "Maximum fuel efficiency requires high altitude. We will be very visible to all hostile air defence systems."

The briefing officer looked over his shoulder to the quiet man in the dark glasses who nodded his head. Then he turned back to the men in front of him.

"This mission will be supported by a full effort of the Israeli Air Force. As I speak, units are being prepared for strikes on targets in Egypt, Libya, Tunisia and Morocco. All air defence radar, missile sites and airbases will be hit. They will not have the time to deal with you." He paused. "British systems and bases on Cyprus and Gibraltar will also be hit at the same time." The pilots looked at each other and all knew the significance of what this operation would mean but they did not ask to be told the reason.

The briefing officer continued to speak. "You will blend in with what will be very busy traffic." He waited for his words to take effect. "However, you will be carrying maximum external fuel so there will only be two air-to-air on each aircraft. It is the job of the wingmen to ensure the lead aircraft survives to hit the target. It is almost certain that Adolf Hitler is a passenger on that plane!"

iv.

"Where is he now?" asked the Prime Minister. The intelligence officer glanced at his watch. "Over Niger," he replied.

"Why is he flying on a scheduled passenger service?"

"Our best guess is for protection. He's using the other passengers as a human shield."

"Who is the risk from?"

"Our assessment would be the Israelis. The Americans and Russians are more likely to stay within international law but the Israelis would not hesitate to intercept that plane if they were sure that he was on it."

The Prime Minister knew his history. Israel did lean out aggressively from within its narrow borders to assert its interests and protect its people, ignoring the laws and sovereignty of other states; Eichmann kidnapped from Argentina in 1960, surprise air attacks against Arab bases in 1967, the 1976 raid on Entebbe, the 1981 air strike on the Osirak nuclear plant in Iraq, the kidnapping of Mordechai Vanunu from Rome in 1986 and, in 1990, the murder of Gerald Bull in Brussels.

"Do they know he's on that flight?" asked the Prime Minister.

The intelligence officer paused briefly before answering.

"Mossad will know he's moving. They may not know the full plan but they will have worked out all the scenarios. We have to presume that the Israelis want him dead or alive and they may well be prepared to bring the plane down."

"Do they have the capability?"

"Oh yes," said the intelligence officer. "Their air force is able to put combat aircraft over the Straits of Gibraltar. That's nearly two and a half thousand miles from Israel."

"Have they made any moves?"

"There is something happening at their bases. Tight security, wide cordons, movement from dispersal. We have a Boeing AWAC watching their airspace. Nothing has come out so far."

v.

The first wave of aircraft lifted off from the tarmac of the

Israeli airfield, bombed up to hit British air force, air defence and radar targets on Gibraltar. They would use the IAF air-to-air refuelling capability somewhere over the Mediterranean.

The Israeli defence ministry had notified the Americans, but not NATO, that the operation was an exercise. It had been calculated that the notification from a friendly power would not be forwarded to other NATO members with much haste or priority, and the British would remain unaware of the planned movement of so many aircraft.

The second wave lifted off heading for Cyprus. Other waves of jet fighter bombers took off at times synchronised with the initial strike on Gibraltar. The three F16 interceptor aircraft took off, camouflaged by the hive of activity of the Israeli Air Force. A radar operator on an American aircraft carrier in the eastern Mediterranean said to his colleagues, "Looks like a hornet's nest poked by a stick."

vi.

The RAF AWAC was the first victim. The big Boeing exploded at 35,000 feet just outside Israeli airspace, hit by air-to-air gunnery at close range. The crew died unaware of any threat. American notification had been that all IAF activity was a legitimate exercise.

The British did not realise that the loss of contact with the AWAC was catastrophic for another few minutes and, even then, did not recognise the loss as due to hostile action from Israel.

As the bombs fell on Gibraltar and Cyprus, attacks went in on air bases and missile sites in Egypt, Libya and Tunisia. Deadly accurate. The three interceptors could now have a free run across North Africa tracked, possibly, by surviving radar but unmolested by hostile aircraft. They would intercept the BA flight somewhere over Tunisia.

vii.

Two F1 Tornados on a live firing exercise in Sicily and a few Sea Harriers on board the through-deck cruiser HMS Invincible were now the main air assets that the UK government could call on in the region.

HMS Invincible had not been targeted by the Israeli strike because she had been part of a United Nations task force providing air support to UN peace-keeping troops in Kosovo. To attack Invincible would have meant dealing with the mainly American destroyers that were the air defence pickets of the task force.

Invincible carried a force of eight Sea Harriers of which five were available for operations, two at immediate readiness. The commander of HMS Invincible was ordered to despatch these Harriers to meet and escort the incoming BA flight. The Invincible's three remaining Harriers would maintain combat air patrols over the ship to protect her from attack.

The Harriers had half the distance to the intercept point than the Israeli interceptors. But, due to the earlier take off time and greater speed of the F16s, the two sets of aircraft would arrive at the same time.

The United States Marine Corps had found that the Harrier could outperform F14 Tomcats in close-air combat exercises below 20,000 feet and the RAF and Fleet Air Arm had also used the Harrier with great success as an interceptor against the Argentinean air force during the Falklands war in the South Atlantic in 1982. The sub-sonic Sea Harrier had a very high thrust-to-weight ratio which gave it many characteristics of a supersonic fighter. The Israeli Air Force interceptors now had some opposition.

viii.

As Israeli aircraft began their return flights from around the region, they started to encounter hostile intercepts from NATO aircraft responding to the UK government's demands for action from its allies.

The two British Tornado fighters in Sicily were half an hour away from being able to take off. They had not been at instant readiness, but had been operating to the schedule of the live fire exercise and had not been due to fly for another three hours.

The pilots were receiving a telephone briefing from COBRA, but the Italian authorities were not happy that the British aircraft were operating under direct British and not NATO jurisdiction. Only high level government-to-government representation got clearance for them to take off. They were to rendezvous with the BA flight from South Africa and escort it into safe air space.

ix.

The BA 747 had not entered Tunisian air space. There was nowhere suitable for an emergency landing and the pilot had been ordered to alter course to the west. The aircraft was now over the Sahara desert in Algerian airspace. The old man sat comfortably in his first class seat, a half-smile on his face, sipping mineral water from a glass as he tried to make his mind up of which option to choose from the vegetarian menu.

x

The Sea Harriers were at the point over Tunisia where the 747 should have been when the F16s' combat radar locked onto them. The Harriers' own defence systems detected the lock-on, alerting the pilots. A series of combat manoeuvres began supported by electronic counter-measures to block hostile radar and hot flares to draw heat-seeking missiles away from the exhaust outlets of the aircraft.

The pilots of the three F16s, after their extended flight over the desert, knew that they did not have the fuel to engage the Harriers in a manoeuvring dogfight. They had been ordered to down the 747 only after visual contact. This was not out of any concern to preserve innocent lives but to ensure the acquisition of the correct target. There could be no repeat of this operation. The 747 had to be found.

A brief flurry of radio talk and the lead F16 half-rolled onto a new course and began climbing away from the incoming British aircraft. The other two aircraft were now carrying out their orders to ensure the survival of the leader.

The four pilots headed towards each other at a closing speed of nearly Mach 2 with ten miles between them. Not yet in visual contact, their training and professional detachment kept their minds on the operation of their aircraft rather than allowing them to dwell on the prospect of their own mortality. They remained cool, not afraid, mentally occupied and sure that there were none better than them, as are all men who choose to face deadly danger. To believe otherwise is to give victory to the opponent.

The first brace of missiles streak out towards the British aircraft. A distant flash as a Harrier explodes in the blue sky high above the desert. Visual contact. Close-quarter dog fighting. Now the Harrier is not at a disadvantage. Multiple flashes from its weapon pods spit 40mm shells towards the F16 which has fired its missiles. Another explosion as the shells tear the aircraft to shreds. No time for fear, no time to eject, the pilot dies with only the briefest moment to realise that he has lost.

Like medieval knights in a joust, the two remaining aircraft streak past each other. The Harrier easily turns onto the tail of the remaining F16. The pursuer now pursued.

But he is too fast for the Harrier. He can outrun him. He has fulfilled his task and allowed his leader to get past this obstacle. The Harrier launches its missiles. The F16 pilot burns precious fuel and flares his aircraft's after burner, giving a few seconds of high intensity boost. The F16 outruns the missiles which, with their fuel spent, drop to Earth like the sticks of rockets on bonfire night. Now, with not enough fuel to rejoin the flight leader, the F16 heads for the deck to make a low level, high speed escape to the ditching point.

xi.

American naval aircraft, operating under NATO orders, fly

in excess of two hundred sorties against Israeli air defence systems.

Radar, store depots, and airfields are severely hit. In 1967, at the start of the Six Day War, the Israeli Air Force suffered losses of about ten percent. That was after many years of meticulous planning and rehearsals. This operation had been thrown together, not completely without planning, but without the detailed preparation needed.

Of the two hundred Israeli fighters, bombers and support aircraft that took part in the raids, more than half were destroyed over the blue waters of the Mediterranean Sea or the dry desert sands of North Africa.

xii.

Using intelligence from a US satellite, which allows the IAF to monitor all flights from potentially hostile Arab states, the remaining F16 is vectored towards its target. It will not be long before the Americans cut the information flow from the satellite. The target radar shows the 747 as a distant blip heading west.

The passenger plane and the five hundred people on it are now within missile range. But the Israeli pilot does not fire. His orders are to make a visual confirmation of the target aircraft before destroying it.

The target is slightly higher than him and moving

away. The pilot knows that he no longer has enough fuel to make the intercept and reach the ditching point. If he is to carry out his orders his only option will be to eject into the desert, within the borders of a hostile people. An image of his wife and daughters flashes into the pilot's mind.

The pilot knows that if he fires his missiles now, the target will be destroyed. He has a chance to get home. If it is the wrong aircraft, innocent people will die. If it is the right aircraft, innocent people will die. He knows that this operation can never be carried out again.

He knows that, in all probability, the target on his radar is the plane carrying Adolf Hitler. This is the only chance in history, in all of time, to bring about justice for the Jewish people, to deliver the sentence called for by the state of Zion.

His finger presses the button to arm the missile. The computer has relayed the target co-ordinates. All he has to do is push the release button and Adolf Hitler, along with hundreds of innocent people, will die. But there is no more time. He feels a massive blow to his body and then nothing.

At 35,000 feet, the F16 disintegrates. A ball of orange flame trails smoke as it falls into the desert.

xiii.

A voice comes through on the 747's radio. "Hello Bravo Alpha, Zero, Zero, Five, Five. This is RAF Tornado." The voice gives the 747 a new course to follow. And then, to the mission control:

"Hello Papa, this is Foxtrot Zulu One. Heads-up no hostiles, over."

"Roger that, Foxtrot Zulu One. Estimate rendezvous with tankers in thirty, that is three zero, minutes. Over."

"Roger, Papa. Out."

xiv.

Egyptian, Syrian and Jordanian forces are on the move to exploit the changed status quo. To take back land that was once theirs, to redraw the old borders.

Israel has lost air superiority. The eyes of the US intelligence service are no longer spying for it. US military and diplomatic support cannot now be openly given. Israel is weakened and once more has to fight Arab armies on three fronts. But these are modern Arab armies who have learned the lessons of history.

xv.

The smoke of war rises from half a dozen countries around the Mediterranean. In London, the Prime Minister, the Foreign Secretary and the Defence Minister sit exhausted in plush leather chairs.

"What do you think he wants?" asks the Prime Minister.

"I think he already has it," replies the Defence Minister. "Old allies at each others' throats; destruction of the state of Israel, regional and, possibly, global conflict."

"But he knows that the UK will protect his human rights," adds the Foreign Secretary. "He's probably got Pinochet's legal team!"

In the corner of the room a television shows a twenty-four hour news channel. The sound is quiet but not right down. The female newsreader talks in a serious voice. "The BBC has just learned that an aircraft carrying Adolf Hitler will land at Heathrow airport within the next forty-five minutes. The Army has been ordered to set up an area of martial law around the airport."

"How did they get hold of that?" asks the Defence Minister. But he knows the answer. Israeli secret service operatives have briefed the British media. There will be a vicious war of spies now, on the streets of London.

"What do you think our next step should be?" asks the Foreign Secretary to the Prime Minister.

"Well," replied the Prime Minister, "I suppose we should send a car to the airport to pick him up."

Heroes For One Day

Aís

A tribute to Keith Laumer's *Retief of the Corps Diplomatique Terrestrienne.*

"Officer on *deck*!"

Everyone in the squad room shot upright, each coming to immediate attention. The end result, however, was more like a storeroom of randomly deposited mannequins than a combat-ready unit prepared for any eventuality.

"Walerian, you utter dingbat! Since when is a sergeant considered an *officer*?"

The room as a whole relaxed as everyone turned to face Roscoe stood there in the doorway. Without any real conviction he just glowered back at Walerian O'Toole, the biggest man in the company and next-in-command after himself.

In response, Walerian shrugged. 'Sorry, sarge, just my joke on the lads; worth it to see their faces, though."

Roscoe Tangier gave a slow sigh then a nod. "I know what you mean – precious few officers ever come through our door." He thought back briefly. "Just the one really, and he was your brother-in-law."

Walerian grinned affably. "Well, no orders to give would explain that. Our talents aren't needed since the war ended the day before we graduated from academy."

Ross moved forward, signalling his men to gather around. "Yup, eight months of total nothing, not even guardian duty. The Planetary Assault Commandos aren't needed anymore; we PAC-men are just too specialised."

"That was yesterday, though. Today I found us something to look forward to; so all that is going to change."

He had their attention.

"In twenty days time we begin our re-training for a regular IS Rangers unit. The 1803rd has agreed to pick up our contracts and we'll be going to capital sector, their home base. That's a pretty fine assignment I got us there, lads. I hope you all appreciate that."

Expressions of hope ringed him, and Ross was satisfied that the choice he'd made had been good.

"In the meantime, we need to report with full gear to ship's Central Allocations."

"What..."

"I don't understand..."

"Exercises...'kin why now?"

Ross met their confused, dark looks with a grin.

"Because we have an accommodation, pre-paid,

ten day pass for Lagri-Shan; vacation world extraordinaire! We just need to turn in all our gear and a transporter will take us away for some serious relax-*elation*!"

He grinned a little more. "It will feel damn good to get away from these puke-yellow walls. A stretch free from ship life will do us good, eh lads?"

"But sarge, what about our Battle-AIs?"

The question from amongst the ring of hopeful faces completely caught him out.

"Umm, they will be re-assigned too; more than likely kept here onboard the *Thor* – all ready for the next bunch of aliens who fancy taking over what we've got. Why do you want to know, eh, Jol?"

Aesir Jolins shrugged uncomfortably, looking a bit embarrassed by the attention as everyone turned to look at him.

"Well, I *am* the Tech Specialist, so I feel a bit responsible for them, that's all..."

"Absolutely no need to stress yourself, they'll be just fine. No one gonna melt them down or anything crazy, so just back up now and relax."

Ross looked around the room for any more questions.

"Right then, gear up you lot and let's get ourselves *vacated*!"

Lagri-Shan is indeed a beautiful world. It gives weight, scent and a better understanding of how care should be taken when using such a word.

Ross shaded his eyes to look across the glowing, pale turquoise of the cove's waters. It was almost completely enclosed by towering swathes of rich foliage, draped like frozen waterfalls from a three-hundred-degree arc of high cliffs towering around him.

I had no idea that so much tonal difference existed even within one colour.

Overhead, Lagri-Shan's azure sky, with its ghost pale rings, added a most direct flavour of otherworldliness to it all.

He was content and at peace, standing there alone on the rippled expanse of fine, glittering beach. With each turn of his head it refracted back a soft rainbow shimmer.

His transport bobbed off to one side, a sleek study in design aerodynamics, something which apparently required it to be burgundy and yellow ochre in equal measures. Other than that, the air-car waited inoffensively enough for when he was ready to return from this current pause in his open tour.

It was only their fourth day on the planet, yet Ross had already left the rest of them to get on with carousing among the host and hostess 'droids. His men, on the other hand, were too busy playing the part of war heroes on leave to notice.

Ross preferred some variety in his pleasures, so he'd started with a two day tour of the nearby islands. Next week he'd make a flight out to the southern continent and tour that too; or maybe it would be the northern one, he still hadn't decided.

He'd begun pondering the more immediate question of what he should eat for lunch when his com-link beeped politely. Everything on this world remained polite and erudite in its interactions with the guests.

"Ross, I am sorry to disturb your solitude." The skimmer AI's voice in his ear-bead was calm. "I must inform you that a severe weather warning has just been issued. We are advised to return to the resort immediately."

"Bad weather, eh, Francis. I thought this world had only one kind at this latitude; namely sun, sun and more sun...?"

"Indeed, I must say it is unusual. We should really do as advised however, even if it is just as a precaution."

"Damn it!"

"Indeed again. Shall I come and fetch you?"

"How long do we have?"

"I am afraid the warning did not specify. Perhaps sooner would be best, for your safety."

"If you say so, but I guess it *must* be bad if a luxury vessel like yourself isn't expected to weather this safely. I thought you were the best available?"

"My manufacturers made me incapable of false modesty; I do however agree with you that there is no skimmer to compare with my class."

"Then what about the resort? If this storm is going to be that bad, aren't we going to be in just as much danger there? Surely you could outrun it."

"Most assuredly – yet I do have my instructions to return you to the resort. I believe a deep shelter was installed during the war, just in case."

Ross nodded and sighed. "Okay, come and pick me up."

He watched the skimmer rise, execute an elegant mid-air pivot and then land itself next to him with a minimum of fuss. He stepped into the sumptuous passenger cabin and strapped himself in.

"I would think it galls your sense of pride, though; you must have some of that, right?"

"Most certainly, but I think of how much damage to my beautiful skin I will be avoiding. Unnecessary time in the garage can be so tedious, trapped amongst the lesser transports."

Ross gave up and waved his hand in the general direction of the resort. "Okay, home then, umm...Francis.

How long before we get there?"

The skimmer complied, lifting with an even surge of acceleration. "Eighteen minutes and thirty eight seconds at optimum altitude and acceleration."

Distracted for the duration by a short film and some fine nibbles, he didn't see what was happening ahead, until the skimmer lurched unprofessionally and went into a bucking descent.

Trained reflexes took over and he struggled with his seatbelt, needing to see what was happening. It felt like a combat re-entry.

*

"Hey there, sarge, enjoy your little sleep?"

Blearily he looked up to see Walerian peering down at him, a worrying level of concern on his features.

"What the hell are…?" He was about to add *…you doing in my room,* when he saw that they were in the hotel's expansive foyer, and he was lying on one of the tasteful, low sofas. His head by then had caught up with his memories, so Ross guessed that things during his absence had somehow gone very wrong.

"How long was I out?"

"Standard neuro-pulse hit, say half an hour."

"Any more Intel?"

"Well…you know how we really wanted to see some action? It seems like Lagri-Shan just got itself invaded right under our noses. We are right at the centre of things, but the only problem is...we haven't got any weapons."

Ross groaned as he moved, more from the post-stun nausea than the situation. "Anyone hurt?"

"No, it went down as a total surprise. They were on the ground with their weapons out, busy rounding everyone up before we had a clue. They must have rigged up a drop-ship to look like a luxury shuttle."

"Who are they, Quenticks?"

"No sarge, some other type of intergalactic ugly. An unknown, I think. There seem to be about three companies of 'em in all; an expeditionary force, by the looks of things. They have us all holed up here, only showing themselves when any stragglers, like you, are dropped off."

"Ahhh, *Hell*."

"Ya, I know what y'mean."

"This isn't going to look good for us once the Rangers get here to clear up this mess."

"I suppose not - unless you've got a plan, eh, sarge?"

"I was picking up seashells less than an hour ago...not thinking about what I'd do in case some homicidal aliens turned up around the next rock."

Walerian looked a little shocked at this admission.

"Well, at least you still had your normal clothes on. Attempting combat in tropical swimwear would not look good."

Ross raised an eyebrow and paused to take in the corporal's stocky body. It was barely concealed under a fine, silk dressing gown; one clearly meant for someone of a slender, more feminine build.

"And your own clothes…?"

"I don't seem to recall where they got to, sir."

Ross didn't pursue it, instead glancing around the big space with its planters of exotic shrubs that divided it all into alcoves of sumptuously furnished ambience. It was an effect spoiled by the large group of captives, for the most part listlessly milling about. Many of them were old, and none looked capable of savaging more than a canapé, or possibly an underling.

A third group, 'droids and a few human resort staff, stood apart from the rest and looked equally lost.

He guessed, in total, that they numbered around two hundred together; it was a hopeless situation.

"Anyone come up with ideas?"

None of his squad wore encouraging expressions.

"I did." Jolins appeared, looking vaguely conspiratorial as he moved closer. "Though I don't want us to get in any trouble for this…" he added.

"For what? And how could it be any worse for us

than being held captive by a hostile force without much chance of rescue?"

The tech specialist leant in a little closer. "I don't mean *us*, us – but me and...*someone* else. We aren't as completely defenceless as you might think."

"Enough of the suspense, this is a combat situation, not the pitch session for a mystery film!"

"We have a Battle-AI with us. I sort of smuggled one down here."

Ross sat up sharply. "You did *what*? How, it's a bit big for personal luggage, isn't it?" He looked at the Tech-Op, unsure what he should make of his insane claim.

"Don't tell me you hacked the luggage manifest again."

Jolins ignored the bait, licking his lips as he pulled out his Personal Tablet. "Hand luggage is about right. She's in here..."

"She?" Ross couldn't help the question.

"Unit D-041. She was curious about life outside, wanted to experience it for herself; especially as she is to be mothballed indefinitely. So I downloaded her core essence onto my tablet. I was going to re-upload her once we got back."

"Her?"

"D-041's personality...it seems quite feminine to me, sir."

Ross looked him up and down, trying hard to ignore the smirks on the others' faces. "I'm glad you have bonded so fully with unit D-041 – though I fail to see how a Battle-AI's personality, female or otherwise, can help us! It's the big guns and smart rockets protected by an extra thick, thick shell of armour that would be of more use to us right now."

Ross got up and paced in a tight circle. "I don't suppose by any chance you lied and *she's* up there in orbit, just waiting to drop in on our new friends and wreak some massive vengeance on them?"

"Sarge, be careful or you'll hurt her feelings!"

Ross gave a covert glance at the Personal Tablet. It was powered up. His shoulders slumped. *This is all too much to deal with in one sitting,* he thought.

"How did you get a whole personality onto a tablet's memory, surely there's not enough room?"

Jolins smiled. "That's better, sarge, she felt quite flattered by that. Truth is, I could download the entire squad's personalities and all its memories without using much space. A century year old adult takes just 10gb of organic memory to store, Lola took double that."

"Lola..." He couldn't shake the image of a dancing nymphet for some reason.

"From a very old song, sarge – well, she isn't really a girl, is she?" He looked around pleadingly. "C'mon guys, what kind of person do you think I am?"

Ross held up his hands in placation. "Right, *Lola*. So just tell me how *she* can help us, even without her guns and stuff."

Jolins in turn stared back at him, his dark eyes motionless as he stretched the silence to a full three seconds.

"I don't believe this. None of you actually learned much about the Battle-AIs, did you? It's far more than a heavy piece of mobile support artillery which can think for itself. They all have full command/interface ability with anything more complex than a household toaster – no pun intended. In combat we can use them to subvert an enemy's automated systems from within."

"Still not understanding..."

"Lola's personality already has control of the hotel's central systems and certain of its peripheries." He indicated the group of 'droids stood with the employees; they all waved back cheerfully. "She knows exactly where the enemy are, their numbers, all comms frequencies and enemy movements; she's even begun work on cracking their comms-codes. Add to that her tactical database and we can turn this situation around to our favour, even get a message out to the nearest Ranger base. This means all we have to do is make sure we are in a position to help our lads once they get here."

Jolins was looking a bit wide-eyed and crazy, but they all saw the beauty of his plan as it blossomed inside their own imaginations, images of true heroic deeds and action jostling aside any inconvenient concerns.

"It's what we were trained to do." His last words were a whispered plea.

"*Hell,* yeah!" Came Walerian's seconding of the motion.

*

Half an hour later, Ross watched the five approaching aliens warily as they drifted confidently into the foyer.

These were indeed a new kind of ugly, or so he suspected underneath their smooth, ovoid space armour. They were also quite small, apparently the norm in these circumstances according to their training; small, mean-spirited, numerous and heavily-armed.

"Are you ready, Jolins?" He had already addressed the other guests and staff, getting them to agree to his plan for affecting a rescue. Mostly this involved them staying out of the way, so hopefully none of them would mess that up too badly.

"Backup in position now, sir."

Behind the invaders, four of the hotel's servant 'droids filed in, each carrying what looked like a tall pile of fluffy poolside towels and bathing robes.

"This had better work..." Ross muttered.

Arranging themselves in a professional-looking spearhead formation, the aliens halted a few metres inside the doorway.

"ATTENTION, CAPTIVES! WE NOW HAVE ALL OF YOU IN CUSTODY. CONTROL OF COMMUNICATIONS ON THIS WORLD IS OURS TOO, SO EXPECTATIONS OF RESCUE ARE TO BE CANCELLED.

"TO BE SURE THAT NONE TRY CONTACT WITH THE OUTSIDE USING A CONCEALED DEVICE, YOU WILL NOW REMOVE ALL CLOTHING AND ACCESSORIES. WE HAVE BROUGHT YOU OTHER THINGS TO WEAR."

At a signal from the invaders, all four 'droids moved forward.

In a blur of motion, too quick for the captives to see, each one flung and then wrapped a big towel around the nearest alien to them. Sensors blocked by the thick fabric, none of the invaders had time to react.

Without waiting, the 'droids swung them around, binding the whole group swiftly with mono-filament wire into an inward-facing cluster; all their weapons aimed point-blank at their leader in the centre.

It was all over in less than a second.

Ross nodded, impressed. "Are their comms blocked?"

"Affirmative, sir; their own jamming field is set up around the building as security precaution. The hotel network has now turned on its own privacy system over the foyer area too. It's better than any military stuff I've seen. Some pretty rich folks come here and so want to be certain no one can snoop in on them."

"Good work, Jolins, and you too...Lola," he added quietly. The tablet just gave a standard *beep*.

The Tech-Op in turn gave a strange wink. "She's maintaining deep cover, sir."

"Right," Ross stood up. "Time to have a little chat with this lot, then." He and his men walked over to where the servant 'droids had apparently spot-welded the aliens' suits to the floor. He looked at them with increased respect, surrounding the alien group in a ready silence, postures still managing to look refined as they waited for the next command.

"Thank you gentle-AIs, each of you did a far better job than most Ranger 'droids I've seen in action – well done."

He walked around the aliens until he was facing the commander between two of his squad. Ross could only assume that this was the 'face' side, as it had three slight protrusion blisters in evidence there that weren't apparently weapons pods.

"From your little speech just a minute ago, it is plain

that you understand our language. What I don't know is who you are, or why you chose to invade Lagri-Shan. Shall we start with you answering those two questions?" Ross looked down on them, admiring the 'droids' grasp of psychology in choosing to pin the captives lower down than they already were – something that he guessed would be especially effective against such a diminutive enemy.

The sounds he got for an answer seemed to confirm this, a broken stream of crackles and spitting sounds that almost sounded like spluttering.

"Well okay. Perhaps as a species superior to ours, you don't feel obliged to answer any of my questions."

"CORRECTNESS!"

Ross kept his expression neutral. Inwardly he grinned at having rattled them into a natural response. It gave him more to go on, but not quite enough; so he pushed further.

"In that case, I shall have no choice but to start finding out my answers in a less polite manner. Do not forget how easily we overpowered you, though; not bad for an inferior species, an unarmed one, too."

"ABJECTNESS OF TRICKED HUMILIATION..." The tone was unhappy.

He let that sink in some more before continuing. "I think I should add that your comms will not reach outside this room. So do not expect any rescuers to come looking for you, at least not in time."

More of the spluttering followed, but nothing else. He would have to try harder, it seemed.

Ross turned and made a cryptic gesture to Jolins, then returned his attention to the commander. "There is a suite in this hotel which has been adapted for all kinds of environments. In there I can peel you from those suits to see who we are dealing with."

"UNNECESSARYNESS! OUR...CO-OPERATION IS ASSURED, INFERIORLING!"

Ross smiled openly now, suspicions confirmed. They had been using prepared speech to address their captives with, but when provoked they reverted to type. These new aliens clearly knew Galactic Standard, so why use recorded demands, unless it was to fool their captives, to mislead them? Now he was determined to find out who they really were, and what they wanted.

A crazy notion formed in his head, based on a fragment of memory from his academy classes. It gave Ross an idea of what he and his men now needed to do.

*

Using Lola's link with the resort's central AI, they quickly moved the guests and staff undetected to the nearest sauna. Thermal camouflaging was a major factor in its favour. Ross was still going on his hunch, but if correct he knew the steam-room would be the last place the invaders would look for their missing captives. He also felt that a little steam might actually improve some of the more desiccated guests' appearance.

His men gathered in the heating plant behind the sauna, another precaution against premature detection. Now it was a question of timing, and of bringing certain elements together before they could go in on the offensive.

In the meantime their five captives, he was certain, would stay undetected. The ever-resourceful 'droids, together with Lola, had come up with an inverse Trojan ploy for them. A crate had been swiftly erected around the captive group then covered with authentic-looking stickers. To any casual observer it would look just like a shipment of luggage waiting there, ready for storage. His hope was that the universal principle of manual labour would ensure no one touched the crate, as it wasn't their job to do so.

"Right, let's have a look at what they're up to right now." Ross looked over Jolins' shoulder, as Lola brought up a series of direct feeds from the central AI's directory.

With some fine tuning, they got a good view of what looked like the main force holed up in one of the resort's elegant bars. Several of the ovoid suits were open, though none of the feeds would give him a clear shot of the occupants.

"So, who are those jokers?" one of his men asked quietly.

"Jag'Quop." Ross said it casually.

"I don't see any Jag'Quop – not one of them *doughnuts* in sight." Walerian was squinting at the screen, sounding a little unsure.

"No, but I'll bet a year's salary that nestled inside those egg-suits, that's exactly what you'll find."

"Sergeant Tangier is correct." Lola spoke through the tablet's voice interface. "Jag'Quop vocal patterns have been detected."

"What are they saying?"

"Unfortunately, I cannot tell with more than a 38% certainty. There is too much distortion from peripheral noise. A plan though, has been referred to several times."

"Why would they invade us now, after so long? Those eight-legged psychos were beaten fair and square over a hundred-and-twenty years ago, before being told to stay away until they could behave properly," Walerian muttered.

"Well, I suppose we'd better move in and find out, before they get around to doing whatever else it is they intend doing to reverse that outcome."

*

Into the ambient lighting of the large bar, seven of the

service 'droids entered, each pushing a serving trolley stacked full with covered food troughs and drink applicators.

The Jag'Quop command group pivoted their suits to face them. The lead 'droid halted at a respectful distance to announce in fluid Jag'Quopian that *lem-klish* and *lur'jha* had been prepared for their refreshment.

Arranging their trolleys in a wide arc, the 'droids took up serving positions in readiness. Drifting closer, the aliens continued to watch while the 'droids released catches and lifted the covering lids, which unexpectedly released copious clouds of billowing steam.

The Jag'Quop recoiled in shock, rebounding off each other in noisy confusion, milling about, trapped by the advancing vapour.

No one knew why they hated it so much, just that they avoided steam of any kind, even when they were safely suited and protected.

Through the mist, salvos of flaming bottles landed into the confusion, lobbed in rapid succession by the 'droids before any Jag'Quop could recover from the shock.

They added bottles of chemical cocktails into the mix, which splashed across the space armoured figures with precision, causing the concoctions to catch alight impressively.

The room swiftly filled with flames, smoke and noise, into which the 'droids scattered containers of dry ice, just as the sprinkler system began dumping pre-heated water all across the room.

Clouds of heavy vapour erupted broadly, expanding to isolate everyone in the room within seconds, leaving each invader isolated in the chaos.

Two seconds later, steel doors snapped shut across the exits just before the floor fell away, or seemed to. Heavy pistons sucked the entire room downwards in a brutal, emergency descent.

Ten seconds later, gravity came back with a vengeance as the room slowed rapidly, coming to a complete stop in its safety cradle, deep beneath the complex.

With the rest of the resort still in place above them, the invaders' command group was now shut off from the remainder of their force. A simple privacy field above the pit blocked any of their attempts to call in a rescue.

*

At the shuttle terminal a few minutes later, Ross' men gathered in the luggage bay. They had sped across the complex, using the underground supply network which served every structure. Ross nodded, happy as he ticked off the box in his head that said 'always use the local terrain to your advantage'.

He peeked up and around from his position beside the ramp, snatching a glance of the big shuttle squatting less than thirty metres away with its belly ramp open.

"Jolins, where are our carts?"

"Arriving in less than a minute, sir."

"Right lads, you know what to do."

They all nodded silently, every one of them the image of a professional soldier ready for action, if you ignored their slightly grubby bathrobes. Lola had vetoed a quick side trip for more appropriate clothing, having located the remainder of the invasion force scattered around the general guest quarters area. They were doubtless going through the unattended belongings there, being notorious trophy hunters. Speed was now critical; once the invaders discovered that a unit of IS Rangers was on the planet, things would get a lot tougher.

"Time to move," Ross ordered as the train of automated carts stopped quietly and two service 'droids climbed with some attempt at elegance from the lower storage compartment in the first.

Taking their example, Walerian and four men climbed into the last three carts, waiting for Ross before closing the doors.

"Jolins, it's your show now. We'll keep 'em more than busy while you and Lola get the shuttle's systems on our side."

All he got was a distracted nod from the Tech-Op, who was already focused in three-way link mode with Lola and the Resort AI.

Facing his four remaining men, each of them clutching an unlikely piece of resort equipment hastily adapted into a weapon, he added simply: "Protect Jolins."

Climbing into the last cart, Ross hoped he knew what he was doing while the door slid shut on the outside world.

He and his men were virtually unarmed and going up against three, possibly more, enemy soldiers. The lives of his men were completely his responsibility now.

With smooth and quiet acceleration, the train of carts moved off, then climbed the ramp and levelled out for their approach.

Riding on top of the first cart, the two service 'droids would be their first line of distraction. Lola had direct control of both, so would handle any communication with the guards.

Sure enough, they slowed to a stop and Ross could hear a muffled exchange of voices from ahead. Noises of the first carts being opened was followed with more talking. By the tone change, his plan to fill it with valuables had worked.

Time dragged and Ross started sweating heavily, more from tension than the sun's building heat on the cart. Jolins' whispered words of "slight delay" into his earpiece didn't help much.

The minutes seemed to sit around on their arse while the carts just stood out there in the open. By now he had hoped to be inside the cargo bay and busy with Phase Two. He felt a panic rising.

Then more voices came distantly and the cart train started to move forward.

Another virtual hour crept around him after they had stopped again, before Jolins' voice gave them the all-clear.

With quiet, small movements, the six of them emerged carefully from their confinement. Using the carts as shield against the open cargo space, they each got the kinks out and blood rushing to their limbs again before moving forward.

Ross briefly assessed the situation: big belly cargo bay; crew deck and all the rest above. Only from the outside did it look like a regular shuttle; inside it was definitely an old dropship.

Outside he could see two space-suited Jag'Quop on the ramp, their backs to him. Their two 'droids were stood off to one side, ignored for now and doing their best to remain that way.

He glanced back along the cargo bay into its rear, looking for the weapons rack, then did a double-take that ended in a feral smile.

"*Hello, baby...*" He thought. The two guards were over ten metres away, but he didn't want to risk that their external microphones were not turned on.

Signalling for two of his men to follow, Ross crept back into the gloom until he stood beside the wedge-shaped APC. This certainly wasn't old, but a new and dangerous-looking machine. It looked to be modelled on the current ISR type.

He motioned for the two to get in. Now he had some serious backup to ensure they would not be disturbed while about the rest of their business here.

Along with the other three, he unshipped a hand-held weapon and moved forward to the crew access port.

After they were gone, one of the service 'droids moved quietly to a control access panel, plugging its adaptor jack into the ship's systems. Lola flowed in and began to do her work.

First off, an alarm for drive failure began sounding, then asteroid proximity and maximum hull integrity loss.

The mayhem blaring around the flight cabin instantly focused the three aliens lounging around in there.

Second up, a salvo from the APC's goo-guns immobilised the two on the ramp, trapping them in a fluorescent pink splash of contact-drying expansion foam.

Then the flight deck crew each felt a cold weapon muzzle pressed solidly behind their eye stalks. It had been a definite mistake to remove their armour-suit disguises.

At his signal, Lola cut the false alarms and Ross had himself a shuttle, weapons and complete control of the situation on the ground.

All he had to do now was stop the Jag'Quop fleet that was undoubtedly heading toward Lagri-Shan, then mop up any remaining looters.

It was his guess that they intended to establish a staging post for a full invasion fleet. Lagri-Shan's location, close to most of the hub worlds and major routes, was ideally suited for just this.

"Nicely done, all of you. I say we launch this baby and get the rest of the job done quickly, before the rest of them notice!"

*

Five days later Ross was standing on the same cove beach, admiring the peace and beauty around him. Once more he was also contemplating what to eat for lunch. Naturally it was at this point that the skimmer AI alerted him of several vessels' imminent arrival.

He sighed and looked up, seeing a flotilla of armoured shuttles and their escort Interceptors bank loudly into view over the tree-covered cliff tops. From their centre, a smaller shuttle dropped swiftly in a storm of blown sand to land almost beside him.

Six figures, each in their bulky, best uniform armour clumped down the still-descending ramp. Two high-ranking officers and four elite veterans crunched across the sand toward him, looking surreally out of place.

"Sergeant Tangier, I presume. If you are not too busy, the Fleet Marshall would like to ask a few questions concerning a certain Jag'Quop fleet rumoured to be in the vicinity."

Ross saluted. "No need sir, my men and I persuaded them to leave peacefully a few days ago."

That stumped them for a few seconds. Then, with a hiss and hum of well-maintained servos, the officer who had addressed him opened his armoured helmet.

"Nevertheless, he would like to receive a full situation report. Nor is he in the habit of hunting down the men under his command to hear such. He is, however, waiting for you in the shuttle."

Dwarfed in their midst, Ross now wondered at the wisdom of choosing such casually garish clothing for the day. He'd been expecting something like this and now felt he might pay a price for such insubordinate rashness.

Inside the shuttle, the Fleet Marshall stood waiting, also in full dress uniform combat armour. Ross saluted again.

"So, tell me, sergeant, how did you manage to persuade them to go away?"

He should have guessed the conversation would have been monitored. "Fairly easy, sir. Before sending the message to ISR Sec-HQ about the invasion, I realised it would take far too long to assemble a force that could counter them in time. I used the local AIs to mimic military comms traffic. We then moved some asteroids out of the orbital rings, mounting them with power units and retuning their signatures to look like the fleet already had taken up position at Lagri-Shan. My bluff, it seems, worked. They didn't come in any closer, not with their first-wave continued silence apparently supporting that likelihood."

The Marshall looked at Ross for a moment, his expression as smooth and impervious as his armour. "A very good ploy indeed. Well done, sergeant. As to how you achieve all that, I will expect to see every detail in your report."

"Understood, sir."

The Marshall nodded, expression softening. "But that can wait until after your leave is over, Captain." He half-turned and looked ready to dismiss Ross, but instead looked back at him, calculatingly.

"Naturally we cannot allow any news of this to be broadcast. Letting it be known that an attack by an outside force almost succeeded just would not do."

"Yes, sir." Ross saluted again, still more than a little bemused at his suddenly being promoted to Captain.

"We shall leave two capital ships here and a small fleet of support vessels to provide assistance with cleaning up the mess; also to establish a ring of suitably disguised defences to ensure that this sort of thing doesn't happen again. You and your men can come back with them once they are done. That should add a few weeks to your leave, as an official/unofficial reward."

He paused again, and Ross got the feeling that everything so far had merely been a preamble. "Captain, I see from your records that your unit is due for re-training. Once that is over, I will have my Master Sergeant contact you. I think there might well be a place for you and your men under my command – lots of loose-end jobs that need tying up, y'know the sort of thing..."

"Yessir. Thank you, sir."

"Very well, Captain Tangier, dismissed for now."

Ross saluted for what felt like the tenth time, then about-turned smartly and marched back outside onto the beach.

Staying at attention as the shuttle lifted and the flotilla circled back around, he smiled. Even if the war hadn't really got started, they had all been heroes, at least for *one* day.

Let's Get Physical!

Lee Williams

How great is this? We're just two guys getting fit together, hanging out and working on our bodies. Who knows, maybe we'll have some fun while we're doing it! People sometimes say to me, "Herb, what would it take for you to make me a competition-level bodybuilder?" Well, my answer never changes, and it's the same one I gave to you earlier. "Just turn up in your shorts," I say. Nine out of ten people never take that advice, but you're the ten percent that makes my job worthwhile.

Let me start by explaining to you what your muscles do and why you need them:

There are more than six hundred muscles in the body. If you worked intensively on a different muscle each day, it would take you almost two years to get through every one of them. Two whole years, almost. To be honest, though, that's not the ideal way to train.

The ideal way to train is to do exactly what we're doing now. Find yourself a partner, someone you can trust and have fun with, and push each other to higher and greater things. My old training partner, Raoul, used to say it's like a see-saw, only you're both going up at the same time. He was full of great advice like that and we used to have some real good times together. We'd do crunches, squat thrusts, dicky sits, always looking to add a few more reps on the sly so we'd top the other's record. It was competitive, but in a lighthearted way. At the end of a session we'd just sit and laugh, sometimes for hours.

By the way, did you know that laughter works on fifty percent of your primary muscles? It does, but the effects aren't all that great. If you're just sitting around laughing all day, then you should try to work in a few crunches or pull-ups at the same time.

Now, back to your muscles:

See these two little fellas up on your shoulders here, on either side of your neck? They're your trapezius muscles and they help with all sorts of everyday jobs, from press-ups to dumb-bell flys. If you take care of your traps, your traps will take care of you.

Several years ago I had a student called John who trained up all his body, I mean he really pumped it up. He was possibly the second or third most ripped student I have ever had in my gym, but there was one thing wrong with him: he neglected his trapezius muscles. He did it on purpose, wrongly thinking they were a waste of energy when the other muscles could do their work for them. I tried to warn him but he just trained carefully around them until they got buried.

Then one day his wife left him and he turned up late, reeking of pancake mix. Her name was Michelle and she was a waitress down at Hoolio's. I knew she was trouble from the start but you can't say that to a friend, not when he's in love.

So this one day I found him stood in the foyer with his hands by his side, crying. I went up to comfort him and when I put my arms out for a hug I knew something was really wrong. He couldn't lift his arms.

"Shoot, John. Your traps have given out!" I said. I didn't want to say I'd warned him this would happen, because I hadn't. It had never occurred to me.

"They're broke, Herb," he told me. "Everything's broke."

He started to cry in big heavy sobs, but he was sobbing from the top of his lungs and it was putting stress on his traps. Usually he would avoid anything that did this, but now I guess he didn't care.

"Don't do that, man," I said, but I was too late. I heard the popping noises as both traps gave out at once, and what happened next was a sight I would not wish on any gym owner or competition bodybuilder, not even my greatest rival.

He collapsed. I mean he literally collapsed. All those beautiful big muscles, that whole fantastic body, just folded in on itself. There are certain pillars and walls in any building that you just shouldn't knock down, and the human body is like that too.

Until you've looked down at the jumbled remains of a promising bodybuilder, and wondered if you'll ever be able to put him back together, you don't know what it means to be a personal trainer.

That's how important your trapezius muscles are.

Okay, next we're going to take a look at your quadriceps. These are the muscles which run down the front of your thighs. If you buff these up properly, it will look as if you have a roast chicken under the skin on each leg. That's some finger-licking good musculature!

Seriously though, these are some important little guys. Without them you would struggle to manage even the simplest squat thrust or scissor stretch. But you can overwork them, and that can be almost as bad as not working on them at all. That was what happened to Raoul one time.

I remember finding him in agony next to the rowing machines, a terrible grimace on his face. My first instinct was to think, "Wow, he's really buff" – his chest and biceps looked magnificent – but then I noticed something was wrong. His thighs were as skinny as a supermodel's!

"Jeez, Raoul! Where are your quads?" I exclaimed.

He could hardly answer me but he jerked his head towards his arms. It was one of the most incredible things

I've ever seen. He'd been doing handstand push-ups when his quads had somehow come loose, detached themselves from his legs and slid down into his arms. Now they were all tangled up with his biceps. You could see them struggling together under the skin.

On that occasion we managed to massage Raoul's quads back down but you could feel them resisting every step of the way. The problem was that they'd become far too dependant on regular training. Scientists call it 'muscle memory'. When they felt they were being left out, they wanted back in.

Anyway, these days Raoul sticks to a carefully planned workout routine. He doesn't neglect his quads, but he lets them know who's boss. Whatever else you do, you can't start letting your body dictate terms to you. It's *your* body, after all.

Okay, lecture over. I don't want to give you the impression that bodybuilding is a dangerous activity. Like anything, it's only dangerous if you don't have a mentor certified by at least three different authorities, including the American Sports and Leisure Council. But the most important thing is to have fun, and I can't stress that enough.

So let's get started.

See this tub over here. That's my own special blend of competition grease. One part Vaseline, one part motor oil and one part… well, that's for me to know! Just dip your paw in there and get a good handful. That's the way.

You do me first.

Heroes

Lev Parikian

She trailed her hand down his recumbent body, relishing the softness of his skin. A shaft of sunlight angled in through the gap in the curtains and highlighted the downy hairs in the small of his back. She could watch him sleep for hours, his tousled head nestled on her parents' pillow. It felt even more exciting, doing it in their bed while they were away. Weird, somehow, but exciting.

Twenty-four hours till the world came back to them. She intended to use them as well as possible. They had to snatch the joy, hold it close to them at all times. Keep the world at bay.

Nobody understood her like he did.

How had she existed before this? Before him? How was it possible to want someone so much that it hurt?

The ache inside her. It lived with her, nourishing, denuding.

Something from school floated into her head.

Oh, brave new world, that has such people in it.

That was it. That was what it was. A brave new world. Her old world, the one she had left behind when she met him, was for kids. This was grown up, real.

At least school was good for something.

It wasn't true, what Janine had said. She was all, don't trust him, you know the people he hangs out with, you don't want to get caught up with that load of druggy tossers.

It wasn't like that at all. Away from them he was different.

They had talked, at first. Just talked and talked about anything and everything. TV, films, books, music.

School.

That was an area of common interest, for sure. Or lack of interest.

They'd joked about the kind of exam they'd like.

Discuss why you hate school and everything to do with it. Include examples of the biggest losers on the staff. Show your workings. Use one side of the paper only. You may begin.

She'd laughed so much when he said that, her drink came out of her nose. And then he'd taken her chin to wipe it away and looked into her eyes.

And then she knew for sure the path from there.

Two weeks ago, that was all. But she couldn't remember what it was like before that.

Without him, there was nothing. Dead-end school. Dead-end parents, too obsessed with themselves to notice what she was doing. What did they care?

Sometimes life was like a gunfight going on all around her, bullets whizzing about her ears. But when he kissed her for the first time it all stopped.

Or slowed down, at least.

Afterwards he'd played her some of the things he'd been listening to, stuff from his dad's collection, and it had blown her away. Music was so much rawer back then. Strange to think that their parents had listened to this stuff first time round. She didn't see her dad pogoing to 'God Save The Queen' Sex Pistols-style.

But she supposed he had been young once, too.

There was one song that they listened to more than the rest, that really got under her skin. Their song. It was about them, she said.

You're my hero king.

And you're my heroine queen.

And he took a big toke of the joint, looked at her straight, and said do you want to try it?

At first she hadn't got what he meant. And then she made the connection and was scared. And then they talked about it, and he was great, of course he was, and she knew it was okay because it was with him and everything was okay when it was with him.

He'd been absolutely straight with her.

You don't have to do it. And if you don't like it you never have to again. But I promise you, it's the best. The biggest high. Like nothing else. Better than fucking.

Nothing's better than fucking, she said.

This is, he said. This absolutely is.

He'd got it from Jason. Jason was a proper smackhead, did all kinds of stuff all the time, and looked like it, too.

But they weren't going to end up like that, he said. He said he just wanted to share it with her. For their love. And that was what she felt, too. All she wanted was to be with him and share everything with him.

Janine was, like, if it's right without drugs, you don't need them, I don't see why you have to do all that stuff, don't you have anything to say to each other?

Blah blah blah.

Janine didn't get it. Nobody got it.

She'd done E before, and of course they'd smoked, but this was different.

This was real.

She looked at him now. He was beginning to stir.

Hey babe.

Hey.

Shall we?

Yeah.

I want to play that song while we take it. Our song. Put it on repeat.

They went into her room and he put the music on.

That guitar sound. How did they do that?

He extracted the bundle from under the bed and carefully laid out the gear. It reminded her of the chemistry lab, a bit.

But she hated chemistry.

He looked into her eyes.

You're sure?

Sure.

My queen, my heroine.

My king, my hero.

The needle slid in, smooth. She was surprised how little it hurt.

And now she was floating away, the glow inside her. Swimming, soaring, swooping. The fizz of his breath in her ear. Her eyes open to the possibility of everything. He was below her and above her and around her and inside her.

The world stopped.

*

Detective Inspector George Carden manoeuvred his bulky frame up the narrow stairs and stood for a second on the little landing. Master bedroom to the left, bathroom straight ahead, little bedroom to the right. He squeezed past Henderson and took a peek in the main bedroom before moving to the threshold of the girl's room. The whole house was very neat and tidy. Spick 'n' span, his mum would have said. Very much at odds with what he knew he was going to find in the bedroom.

The pathologist was already there.

"You're here nice and early, Jim. What's up? Insomnia?"

Jim Staunton looked up.

"No, George, just devotion to duty. I was going to ask you what took you so long."

"Ah, well. It seems that they were uncertain whether I'd be needed. Were they right?"

"Nothing suspicious so far, except for the use of an illegal substance. Poor lass took some bad shit."

He indicated the needle hanging from the girl's arm.

"On her own, was she?"

"No indication to the contrary so far. You'll want to pass this back to the uniforms, I reckon."

Carden walked into the room and over to the window, sidestepping the prone corpse of the unfortunate girl. He stood for a minute staring out of the window.

"Do you know what I'm thinking, Henderson?"

"Not really, sir, no."

"I'm thinking a young lass like this doesn't take drugs by herself. I'm thinking I can smell something odd, and I'm not talking about your socks."

He turned and looked the young constable in the eye.

"I'm thinking someone else was here."

"Sir…can I ask? How do you know?"

"Well, let me turn it back to you, Henderson, as you're so keen to learn. What do we have here?"

"Sixteen-year-old girl, died suddenly. Indications show she was using drugs, probably heroin."

"Yes indeed. Indications. Great big fucking needle sticking out of her arm and a bag of smack on the bed. But what else, lad?"

"She was discovered by her parents on their return from a weekend away late last n-"

"Don't give me all that shit, Henderson. I can read that later. What actually happened here? Try using your powers of observation, lad. Look around you."

"Well, sir…"

"Yes?"

"Well, sir, I'm not too sure what you're getting at, to be honest."

Carden moved quickly for a large man. He sprang across the room, grabbed Henderson's jacket with one hand and the seat of his trousers with the other, and propelled the hapless constable outside, across the landing and into the master bedroom.

"Now, then. What do you see?"

"A bedroom, sir."

"And the bed?"

"Unmade, sir."

"And on the floor?"

"A condom, sir."

"Now, then, Henderson, using your magnificent powers of deduction, for which you are renowned throughout the force, would you say that said condom was likely to be used or unused?"

"Well…"

"So we have an unmade double bed in the master bedroom. Fair enough. Mr. and Mrs. Johnson might have left in a hurry for the weekend. And a used condom on the floor. Less likely but still possible. Perhaps passion got the better of them and they had a pre-breakfast quickie on their way out. But you tell me this, Henderson. Would you say this house was in the 'messy' camp or the 'tidy' camp?"

"Tidy, sir."

"And would you say, on the basis of what you have seen so far, that Mrs. Johnson is the kind of person who is likely to leave a used condom on the floor when she goes away for the weekend?"

Silence.

Jesus wept, thought Carden. He can't see it. He can't fucking see it. He wouldn't notice a baseball bat swinging towards his head.

"Well, let me tell you what I think, Henderson. It

seems to me, with my vast knowledge of the human psyche and four decades of experience, that the poor lady who is currently sitting downstairs in a state of deep shock at the untimely death of her beloved daughter would rather staple her tongue to the floor with a rusty croquet hoop than leave so much as a used tea bag on her beautiful corian kitchen worktop, let alone a spunky cumbag on her inappropriately-named shag pile."

"Yes, sir."

"Which, in turn, leads me to the thought that maybe it was yon lass in there who was responsible for the crumpled sheets. Doing it in the parents' bed with a boyfriend as yet unidentified. What a thrill for 'em, eh?"

Henderson was in one of his quiet moods.

"And then what do you suppose happened? Our young man lets himself out and she smacks up in his absence? Unlikely, don't you think? No, I'm guessing that he's shot her up, gone into a blue funk when she's OD'ed, done a hasty and not very convincing clear up and is currently sitting somewhere not far from here, shitting bricks and wondering how he got himself into this mess. So what do we need to do now, Henderson? Do we need to stand here pissing the day away while I explain police procedure to you, or do we need to get off our arses, find out who her friends are and talk to them so that we can track down our mysterious smackhead?"

Henderson stood, silent and awkward. He was having difficulty meeting Carden's piercing gaze.

"Sir…I need to tell you something."

Carden did a double-take.

"It talks!"

Henderson appeared to be girding his loins.

"Well, sir…While you were on the way here I spoke to the parents for a few minutes. There's a couple of things. Firstly, there was a song playing on a loop on the iPod when they found the body. Probably not significant but we need to know. David Bowie. '"Heroes"'. The kind of song that would appeal to young lovers who think they can change the world."

Carden was taken aback. Deep insight from Henderson. What next? Rollerskating elephants on the ring road?

Henderson was aware of his boss's surprise but carried on regardless.

"Secondly, the deceased didn't have a boyfriend that they knew of but had seemed happier for the last couple of weeks, although that coincided with her not doing so well at school. And thirdly…"

He hesitated.

Carden cocked a cynical eyebrow.

"Yes, Henderson? Take a deep breath."

"She was at the same school as your son, Jason,

sir."

A heavy silence fell on the room.

Carden looked at the young constable, trying not to let his thoughts show.

He knows, he thought. Sweet fucking Jesus. Everyone knows.

"What are you suggesting, Henderson?"

Henderson stood up straight, made eye contact and held Carden's gaze.

"I'm not suggesting anything, sir. I just thought you should know."

After a few long seconds Carden nodded and turned to walk down the stairs. There was an unaccustomed slump in his shoulders.

"Thank you, lad," he murmured. "Good work."

If you've enjoyed these stories, please visit www.youwriteon.com to read more work by every author featured in *Pop Fiction: Stories Inspired By Songs*.

Read more by Marc Nash at: http://marcnash.weebly.com and www.sulcicollective.blogspot.com

Read more by Lev Parikian at: www.runnythoughts.com

Read more by Daniel Lewis at: http://daaanlewis.com

Lightning Source UK Ltd.
Milton Keynes UK
26 November 2010

163485UK00001B/3/P